Quicksilver Summer

D. Jean Young

Cover art by Dan Clark

ROUSSAN
PUBLISHERS INC.
Specializing in YA and fiction for pre-teens

THE CANADA COUNCIL | LE CONSEIL DES ARTS
FOR THE ARTS | DU CANADA
SINCE 1957 | DEPUIS 1957

We acknowledge the support of the Canada Council for the Arts
for our publishing program.

We acknowledge the financial support of the Government
of Canada through the Book Publishing Industry
Development Program for publishing activities.

http://www.roussan.com

National Library of Canada
Bibliothèque nationale du Québec

Canadian Cataloguing in Publication Data
Young, D. Jean, 1954-

Quicksilver summer

ISBN 1-896184-36-7

I. Title.
PS8597.O588Q43 1998 jC813'.54 C98-900316-7
PZ7.Y68Qu 1998

Interior design by Jean Shepherd
Cover design by Dan Clark

Published simultaneously in Canada and the United States of America
Printed in Canada

1 2 3 4 5 6 7 8 9 AGMV-MRQ 3 2 1 0 9 8

Dedication

To my mother who listened to my first
stories and my father who was always
there when we really needed him.

Quicksilver!!!

Need to know just how hot it really is?
Use quicksilver.

Need to heal a hurt?
Use quicksilver.

Need to store energy in a battery?
Use quicksilver.

Need to set off a bomb?
Use quicksilver.

Need to get gold from ore?
Use quicksilver.

Kill a parasite, make a hearing aid, create a thermometer, trigger a grenade.

Use quicksilver, the quick-moving metal, also called Mercury.

Criminals and tramps asked Mercury, Greek messenger of the gods, to be their heavenly protector.

In a Quicksilver Summer, troubles can explode like a bomb.
In a Quicksilver Summer, old wounds can heal.

CHAPTER ONE

I'm Jason Abbott. Most of my life I've been trying to prove I'm not stun. After this summer, I've also got to prove I'm not a hardened criminal.

It's hard to change a bad name in a small town. Everyone knows—or think they know—everything about you. If you'd asked anyone about me on the last day of school this year, they'd say, "Oh, yes. He's Marsha Abbott's son. She had him when she was real young. He's a bit idle. Doesn't do much in school. He's not really bad."

If you'd asked them what my friends were like, they'd say, "The bunch he hangs around with are all alike. Not much difference in any of them. They're all tarred with the same brush."

Really, that's not true at all.

We were the last kids to leave the schoolyard. Nine of us hung out together. Old test papers filled the rusty, tin garbage can. The wind banged the gate against the chain-link fence.

All the kids with good report cards had hurried home. For once, I wanted to show my mom my report card, too. I'd passed everything for the first time in years and years. Mind you, except for A in art, my highest mark was 60% in math.

No one else in our crowd had passed every single subject. Today I was the star. I knew how the others felt. That's one reason we stuck together. Failing doesn't hurt so much when you're with friends. Even with bad reports, we were free for the summer. Free and easy.

By the end of grade nine, each of us was a couple or more grades behind other kids our age. That's hard. Most of the kids in our class were smaller and younger than us. They thought about things that we dealt with two years ago. The kids we started school with were in higher grades. We didn't fit in there either. In the summer this shouldn't have mattered. But it did.

The guys in our gang all cut their hair short; each of us wore a star earring—right ear. On that last day of school, we added one more piece to our total group look. Vince, a short nervous guy who's hardly ever passed anything, started the ball rolling. He looked at his report card and sighed. "Special Ed again next year." He scrunched up the cardboard form and tossed it into the garbage can. "No one's going to want to see that." He paced around a picnic table. "We need more of a style. So we'll look like we're all together."

"Like what?" Paul asked. He wiped his mouth on his sleeve. He'd just finished a big bag of Cheezies. "It's gotta be cheap."

He had a point. Report card day wasn't a time when we asked our parents for anything. Everyone wore a jean jacket. Most of the jackets had frayed collars and cuffs.

"We'll do something with our jackets. They're worn out, anyway." Elvis pulled off his jacket. He spread it out on a picnic table. He found his compass in his backpack. "This has a good, sharp point. I never could draw circles with this thing. It's gotta be good for something." He made a small hole and tugged. The fabric was still pretty strong.

Jonathan grabbed the jacket. He stood a tiny bit shorter than me, but his muscles were the size of two-litre Pepsi bottles. He stuck two fingers in the hole, gripped and yanked, hard. The whole sleeve ripped all around. He gave the seam an extra tug.

We handed our jackets to Jonathan and Elvis. Pretty soon, we all had jean vests.

Mike handed over his jacket last. While they ripped off his sleeves, he said, "Maybe we shouldn't do this."

Tom and Tony, identical twins, each picked up two sleeves, tucked them into their jeans.

"The latest in alien fashion," said Tony.

"Perfect when you want to hug your girl," Tom added.

"We need a symbol." Joey was stretched out on a nearby picnic table. He stared up at the gathering clouds. "How about a cloud? A mushroom cloud. An atomic bomb cloud."

Here's where I came in. The art teacher had given me a whole bunch of leftover art supplies including paint and brushes. While I painted mushroom clouds and half-listened to the chatter, I thought about school.

"You must be getting good with the pictures, Jason." Vince looked at my report card. "Fifty per cent in English. I figured you'd fail. Especially after Miss Reid lost her false teeth."

I'd passed in a test to Miss Reid one day without a single written word. I'd drawn scenes from the play *Romeo and Juliet*. I hadn't read the play, but I'd seen two videos. She wasn't impressed.

She'd yelled at me; the scalp of her dyed blonde hair turned red. Her teeth flew across the room. Just missed Rodney. He'd never said Boo! in his whole life.

"Well, she said my words were 'Gibberish, pure gibberish!'" I kept painting. "And she said a picture's worth a thousand words. Ah, there's no pleasing teachers. I guess she didn't want to see me next year."

I said that. But my last couple of papers hadn't been too bad. Thanks to Ginny Hope. Ginny had done her internship for a special education degree at our school this year. Miss Turner gave her all the hard cases. The below-normals. The hopeless ones. Kids like me. She assigned her to us one at a time.

Ginny had thick glasses and long, messy hair that flopped around her face or stuck out from a scraggly pony tail. She was about fifty pounds too heavy. At our first meeting, I drew a cartoon of her. I made her look a hundred pounds overweight.

She pushed back her hair and sighed. "Yup. That's how I feel. Give me that, Jason. I'll put it on my fridge. To remind me to stop eating." That's all she said. No lecture. She didn't say the picture was *inappropriate*. She wasn't like other teachers.

She helped me with phonics. (I would have spelled it *fonix* in September.) She helped me with word recognition. I felt stupid tracing out letters and words and repeating them out loud. It helped. Best of all, she said I was smart. Said it like she meant it. She convinced the principal and my mother that my problem was *correctable*.

Deep down, I'd never believed I was dumb. Most of what the teachers talked about made sense. I remembered just about everything. Couldn't read anything though. Kids spit back the words like parrots and passed—kids who didn't have a clue what anything meant. I kept failing. I couldn't put anything down on paper. Jumbled it all up.

I imagined a crowd of Miss Turners in every field. Like the Helens on *Kids in the Hall*, they all waved posters, saying thirty Miss Turners agree, JASON IS STUN!

Even my mother said, "Jason, my son, never mind. None of our crowd was ever good at books. Not me. Not Nan. And mother couldn't even read or write. I never bothered with books. Didn't need to. Didn't want to."

We had lots of videos, but no books, on our shelves. Mom would sigh and say, "Never mind being stun in school, boy. Our crowd always manages."

I don't know my real father. Mom only told me he lives on the mainland. She doesn't want me to bother him. She figures the less I know the better. I wonder if he was good in school. Mom was only sixteen when I was born. Same age as me now. She quit school and went to work as a waitress.

When I was ten, she married George Evans. She asked me over and over if I liked him. I sulked for a while, but then I said yes, he's okay. I don't call him Dad. He wouldn't want that. Sherri, my little sister, is four and a half.

Anyway, thanks to Ginny, I passed grade nine. I gave her another picture before the last school bell rang. Done in pastels on a board my art teacher gave me. I made her look good—her eyes sparkled, had a nice haircut, nice clothes. Most of the time her clothes were too sloppy or bar-tight.

She looked at the picture, looked up at me. "I don't look that good."

I blushed. I'm not used to being nice to teachers. "It's just a thank you, that's all."

She grinned up at me and shook my hand. "Thank you, Jason." She marched down the hallway, carrying her picture. She walked straighter and taller than ever before.

I painted another cloud and wondered where Ginny would be in the fall. Mind you, I didn't turn into a perfect student overnight. I'd slipped up last month. Most of the time, I managed to keep out of major trouble. Oh, sure, I saw the principal now and then. He can't strap any more. I bet he wishes he could. Since I'm a bus student, he couldn't even keep me after school. Seeing the principal didn't matter. Hear one lecture, you've heard them all. I crossed the line last month.

Elvis brought it up. "You know when to get kicked out, Jason. I always liked that about you."

I laughed as I shaded in the underside of the last mushroom. I'd mixed up the wrong chemicals. Almost blew up the chemistry lab. "Mr. Graham said we have to learn by doing." That lesson cost me a three-day suspension.

Elvis cut class. We spent the three days fishing. The weather was perfect. Elvis took our catch home. It took some doing and a few forged notes and unplugged phones. Mom never knew I missed a class. Teenagers never tell their parents everything. Everyone is happier that way.

I looked at my watch. Mom should have her groceries home by now. I wanted to share my good news: promoted with a diploma. I stood up and stretched. Mike admired his cloud. We tossed the torn sleeves into the garbage can and all left together.

I'm a bus student, but by taking shortcuts, I'd be home in half an hour. We put on our vests, wet paint and all. Joey began whistling; we all joined in. It was good to be with friends, free for the summer. We never guessed we were headed for trouble.

CHAPTER TWO

We had no big plans for the summer. Jobs were scarce. At the best of times, guys like us were the last to be hired. None of us expected to go on a major holiday. We'd have our beach fires, long walks, fishing, a dance now and then. Once in a while, one of us would hook onto an odd job. Sometimes, Jonathan worked with his father. Sometimes, he even got paid. Around their pay days, our parents might cough up a few dollars. It wouldn't be a great summer, or a horrible one.

Maybe, if Ted Dawson hadn't come along, that's the way it might have been. We were too broke, too laid-back, to get into real trouble.

Ted showed up with Vince one night. They met us at our usual street corner. Ted was taller than me. And I was the tallest of all of us. Ted swaggered. Like he dared the world to take him on. Something about him put me off. I hated that. I wanted to know why I didn't like him. I could tell he didn't take to me, either.

"This is Ted Dawson. He moved into the house on the hill." Vince introduced us, one by one.

Ted sized us all up and nodded. Like he had us all figured out right away. He didn't say much that first night. Mostly, he just watched us. Around ten-thirty, he said, "Let's get some chicken."

"With what?" Paul licked his lips. "We're all broke."

Ted took out his leather wallet. His name was on it, in gold letters. He yanked out two crisp, twenty-dollar bills. They looked like they came fresh out of a bank machine. "This should cover it."

"We don't want you to pay for everything." I said this while my mouth watered.

"What are friends for? Come on. I'll get a bucket."

We went with Ted. When we sat down to dig in, he asked us questions. "What do you guys do?"

I spoke first. "We don't do drugs. Or get into serious trouble. We don't look for fights. But we don't walk away if someone picks for one."

Ted stared at me. His eyes were like slits. He tore off a piece of chicken skin. Ate it. Slowly. "That's a lot of 'don'ts,' Jason. What do you *do*?"

Jonathan replied. "If someone picks on one of us, he answers to all of us. We can handle ourselves."

Ted nodded. "All for one, one for all. That's good."

Vince chipped in. "Sometimes, we get a dozen beer. Drink around a fire where the river goes into the lake."

Joey hadn't taken a bite of his chicken breast yet. He'd picked it up. Sniffed it. Stared at it. Now, very seriously, he bit into the golden brown skin, through to the white meat. He took his time, chewing it, tasting it. He swallowed and said, "We don't *do* anything special. We take things as they come. Live in the present. What about you, Ted, what do *you* do?"

Ted smiled at Joey. "Right on, man. I see where you're coming from."

Ted joined us at the corner the next evening. We all leaned against the window ledge of One-Hour Martinizing. Heat oozed up from the dusty sidewalk. Cars whizzed by leaving the scent of gasoline. Girls strolled past. We whistled. They made like we weren't there.

Ted strutted up in a new, stone-washed jean jacket. Must have cost a fortune. Our vests were about the same colour. They got that way from a whole lot of washing.

Ted stopped dead centre in front of us. He had a new, short haircut. A star earring sparkled in his right ear. It had a diamond inset. His ear lobe was red.

No one said anything. We watched Ted. Moving slow and sure, he unbuttoned his jacket. In a slick motion, he slipped it off. Next, he moved in toward me and Mike. We split apart, left a space on the cement ledge. Ted lodged his jacket there. From his shirt pocket, he took a pair of surgical scissors.

"The old man's a doctor," he said. Calmly, Ted nipped the right sleeve of his brand-new jacket. He started to cut.

Mom would have killed me.

Ted did the job neatly. The sleeves flopped to the sidewalk. He kicked them out of the way. He tossed the de-armed jacket at me. I moved back from the impact. That jacket felt wrong, like something hurt, like a dead dog.

"Paint the cloud." He said it like I had no choice.

"I don't take orders."

Vince said, "Aw, come on, Jason, give him a break. We're not snobs. We don't turn no one away."

Paul agreed. "Yah. We're not snobs." I guess he was thinking of the chicken. "Don't be a jerk, Jason."

I stood there, holding that heavy, wounded jacket, feeling cornered. I threw the jacket back at Ted. "Drop over to my house in the morning. Maybe, I'll do the cloud then."

Ted showed up around eleven-thirty the next morning. He didn't say much. He smoked and watched me. I painted the spookiest mushroom cloud of all.

I didn't like Ted. But he drew me to him, like we were somehow linked, meant to be together. Over the next few weeks, Ted told us his father had just left the military; this was his first private practice. They were used to moving. Ted fell back a couple of times when he changed schools halfway through the year.

"Most times, though," he told us, "Dad would have a little chat with the teachers. They'd pass me no matter what I did or didn't do."

There were lots of nights when Ted bought us chicken. And cigarettes for the other guys. I don't smoke. Tried it once. Got sick. Besides, the smell of old smoke on clothes turns me off. Smokers don't seem to notice.

Ted always had money. Thanks to him, we had beer all the time now. He had this way about him that made you go along with what he wanted. He could tell a story so you had to listen. Ted was more restless than the rest of us. We let things happen. He made things happen. As we drifted into summer, we went along with him more and more. That bothered me. But it was easy to follow his lead, to go with the flow.

When the time came when we should have stopped him, we didn't know how.

CHAPTER THREE

We drank our beer at the beach. Before Ted, we'd share a dozen. Just enough to drive away thirst while we stretched out around our fire. We often had a two-four now—two each for me, Joey, Elvis, Mike and Ted, one extra for Paul, Jonathan and Vince, and five between Tom and Tony.

Two beer made me the tiniest bit dizzy, but it didn't seem to hurt me. By the time I went home, I was sober as a judge. I chewed Dentyne because I didn't want my Mom to know I drank beer.

Three weeks into the summer, I painted Mrs. Christian's fence and she gave me a twenty. I felt rich. It was my turn to buy beer.

On that dusty, blue-sky evening, I went to Bill's Store. Three different colours of paint peeled off his heavy, wooden door. Bill's Store was dark and dingy. The door creaked shut behind me. I took my time going all the way up to the counter—a whole metre from the door. I looked at the beat-up paperback Westerns stacked in an old wire rack.

Bill leaned back on his old wooden chair, watching me. He picked his yellow teeth with a broom straw. I could smell him. Sweat stains spread under the arms of his stained Blue Jays T-shirt. A three-day stubble covered his face. I don't know anyone who ever saw Bill clean-shaven, but he never grew a beard.

I made it to the counter and rubbed my fingers on cigarette burns, scrapes, carved initials. I took a deep breath. Bill swung his feet off the counter and threw his straw into a white, salt-beef pail.

"Six, a dozen, or a twenty-four?" Bill never asked any other questions. Like "How old are you?" or "Why are you drinking?" We all liked Bill.

"A dozen."

Bill rolled to his feet, quickly, like he was slim and tall, instead of short and fat. He opened the cooler door. Inside, I saw six men in heavy overcoats playing poker around a rickety, wooden table. Beer cases towered all around them. No one looked away from their cards.

Bill picked up a dozen Blue Star. I wanted Black Horse but I didn't tell him that. Bill's no fool; he put my beer in a white, plastic Food Central bag. I paid fifty cents a dozen extra for the underage charge.

I hurried down our one-sided Main Street. The railroad on the other side is scrapped, now. Dirt bikes, ATVs, skidoos, and walkers use the rail bed. Our Main Street looks like it came straight out of a TV Western—old stores, false fronts. Two gunslingers facing off would look right at home.

I imagined a gunfight as I walked along the sidewalk. Snotty Billy Ryan stared at my bag. He's about twelve. He pushed his black-rimmed glasses up his freckled nose. He yelled, at the top of his lungs, "I knows what's in there. I knows where you're going!"

I ignored him, walked faster, almost bumped into Mr. Walters. He must be ninety. He huffed, puffed, poked my chest with his cane. He shook his head at my bag, frowned. "Tut, tut," he wheezed. "Watch yourself, my boy, watch yourself."

A crowd of guys, a bit older than me, leaned against the tavern window. They grinned at me, at each other. They remembered old times, I guessed.

Everyone knew what was in that white bag. Everyone knew where I was going but no one stopped me. It was good to get past Main Street. Too open. Next, I headed down a narrow trail through birch and alders.

I stopped once under a big, old birch. I leaned against the white trunk, smelled the woodsy scents, listened to the silence. Everything seemed far away. A yellowhammer chirruped at me, cocked his head from side to side. Evening sunshine drew patterns on my hands and a sad kind of feeling washed over me, like all the goodness was easy to break, like it couldn't last.

When I'd left home tonight, Sherri sat and giggled between Mom and George while they watched a rented video. When I saw the three of them together like that, I got lonely. I'll never, ever, sit between my mom and my real father. Not like that.

I sighed. The yellowhammer flew away. It was time to get

moving. My friends waited at the riverbank.

We had a private spot. A half-circle of alders made a small room opening to the river that poured into our lake. Right in the middle of the golden sand, we had our fire pit.

Most of the guys were there already. As usual, Vince paced. He seemed more hyper than ever. He kept glancing at me and he'd start to speak. Then he'd stop.

Paul ate from a jumbo size bag of sour cream and onion chips. Joey played with sand. He'd pick up a handful, watch it trickle through his fingers. He sizes everything up all the time and gets interested in the oddest things—like sand. And you find yourself looking at sand in a different way, too. When I was around Joey, I noticed all kinds of different stuff.

Tom and Tony buried Jonathan with scoops of sand. Jonathan just lay there, not moving.

Elvis fished with an alder pole. He always carries a line and fish hook. He cast out his line, watched it drift downriver.

Mike and Ted weren't there yet.

I put the bottles in a little cage we had rigged up offshore. Water kept the beer cold. Someone had a dozen there all ready. We never started drinking until everyone was there.

It was still warm, quiet, perfect for a swim. I stripped to my shorts, ran in, real quick. The river never warms up so it's best to get used to the cold right off the bat. Tom and Tony had finished burying Jonathan; only his face showed. They hit the water at the same time, grabbed me by the feet, pulled me under. I wriggled to the surface, spitting and gasping and dunked Tony. Tom slid under my legs, toppled me. I pulled him under, too. Tony tickled me under my right arm. I didn't have a chance against those two.

Vince tossed in an old antifreeze jug. "Race for it," he yelled. I touched it, Tom grabbed it, they started tossing it back and forth.

I swam in, shivering now, as the sun slipped down past the trees. A quiet breeze whispered through the alders. The sky turned a faded, denim blue, pushed away the gold. I dried off with my T-shirt, pulled on my jeans, the damp shirt and my vest. We always kept our fire pit ready to light. Vince tossed me his Bic lighter. I lit a coil of birch rind. The fire burst into life, slashed tongues of light into the evening darkness.

Vince paced while Jonathan stayed still and silent. Tom and Tony swam in, flung the wet jug on the fire. It sizzled and spit, shrivelled into nothingness. The wet label hissed as it disappeared. Elvis cut his line from the pole, tossed the pole onto the fire.

Suddenly, footsteps crackled through the alders. Everyone, even Vince, got still and quiet. We expected Mike and Ted, but...

Clouds covered the moon. A breeze blew sparks to the north. All of us, except Jonathan, crowded together, backs against the wind, faced the trail. He stayed buried in the sand. We watched the black, empty hole where the trail stared out from the trees.

Ted charged through and Mike trailed. We all relaxed.

The mound of sand quivered. Jonathan stretched, broke out of his cocoon. He bounced to his feet in one powerful movement and stretched. "It's about time," he bellowed. "Let's have a beer!"

Vince rubbed his hands together. "Yes, we'll have a beer. Or two, or more. And then..."

Ted glared at Vince and Vince shut up. Ted and Mike had a dozen Black Horse. That made four dozen. More beer than we'd ever shared. And I was getting a feeling that there was more going on, too, something between Vince and Ted. Something dangerous.

Chapter Four

Most times, people act the same old way. Sometimes, though, things tilt. This night had a weird feeling. Like it was a night I'd want to remember. I went into watching mode.

Mike put his dozen into the holding cage. He wouldn't look at me. He was hiding something.

Ted ripped open his cardboard carton. He passed around bottles. Paul threw his empty chip bag into the fire. He grabbed his bottle. Jonathan took his own bottle. One gulp, and half his bottle was gone. "Aahh! Good!" Tom and Tony traded bottles. Joey held his bottle close to the fire. He watched the beads of sweat form on the brown glass. He held the bottle up. Fire colours shone through the beer. Elvis put his unopened bottle beside him. From his shirt pocket, he took a KitKat and ate the gooey chocolate slowly.

Vince took a short swallow, two more, frowned at Ted. "You said—"

Ted put his finger up in shushing motion.

Mike gripped his bottle. He didn't open it.

As the night got darker and later, we joked, carried on. Every so often, Elvis threw another log on the fire. I twisted the cap of my third beer from the wet, cold bottle. A wisp of vapour floated in the night air. Pouf!

"The genie!" Joey smiled at me. He raised his beer. "To Aladdin and his gang of merry thieves."

Paul and Jonathan downed their fourth bottles. Mike hugged his first sealed beer. Vince had thrown up his first beer; he took his time with the second. Elvis sipped his second. Joey savoured each taste, slowly.

Ted crouched, like a cat waiting to pounce; he drank steadily, calmly, watched us all. When the chatter stopped for a single second, when silence hung over the crackling fire, Ted coughed. We all turned toward him.

Ted reached into his white plastic bag. Slowly, like it was a big deal, he drew out a crumpled, brown paper bag. He crinkled the paper and looked at us. One at a time. He waited until that brown paper bag seemed to be the most important thing in the whole world. Like it held the biggest and best secret. No one said a word.

Joey stared at the bag with wide, dreamy eyes.

Ted ripped the bag. The little noise tore into the silence. Joints spilled onto the soft sand. A rainbow of tiny pills caught on the bottom fold.

"We agreed," I said, "no drugs."

Ted smiled at me. I hated him. "Who agreed, Jason? Vince? He told me Mike could get me a good deal. Mike? He set me up with his brother."

Mike looked away.

"Why, Mike?" I knew. Mike was saving for a car. Next week, he was taking his driver's test. We all knew Mike's brother, Lloyd, was the top pusher in town. Lloyd was six-four, about 250 pounds, had curly, bushy black hair. He'd fade into the background any time a blue-and-white was near. Mike had sworn he'd never get into *The Business*. A friend of his had died from an overdose two years ago. Now, he'd set up a deal!

Paul, Jonathan, Tom and Tony: Mom would say they were all "easy-led." Left alone, or in with anyone half-sensible, they wouldn't get into trouble. They went with the crowd, with whoever seemed the most likely to have a good time. Paul loved smoking, eating, drinking. Jonathan and the twins were game to try anything.

Everything depended on Joey, Elvis and me.

Joey reached across the sand. Touched the paper bag. Picked up a joint. And a pill. Sniffed the scent of the grass. Rolled the pill between his fingers. Stroked the joint like it was a kitten. We watched Joey and waited.

"Okay, Ted. I'll try this. See what all the fuss is about."

Paul, Jonathan, Vince, Tom and Tony fell over each other, grabbing. Lighters flicked. They lit the twisted smokes. The stink of burning rope mixed into the night smells of water, trees and fire.

Elvis jumped to his feet. "Stop this! Jason's right. We don't do drugs." He was too late. Way too late. No one paid him any attention. "Let's stop this." He looked around our circle.

Joey looked him straight in the eye. "You don't have to take any," he said.

Mike sighed, turned away. He sank to the ground, sat with his back to the rest of us. There he sat, rocking, holding his beer. With his arms wrapped around his knees.

Elvis turned to me. No one else bothered to pay any attention to him. "How about you, Jason?"

"I don't want this garbage. Sit down. Keep me company."

He nodded, sat by me. He didn't drink any more. I did. I drank my fourth beer faster than ever before. Ted pushed the tore-up bag at me. One part of me wanted to try the stuff, to see how it worked. Some guys had told me about psychedelic colours, hallucinations. I wanted to see what it would do. How would I feel, what would I see, or imagine?

I didn't want Ted to know I was tempted. I ignored him. Ted smoked in short puffs. He didn't inhale. The other guys sang, bounced all over the beach. Vince raced up and down the short slope of our hideaway. He flapped his arms, and sang, "I can fly, I can fly, I can fly."

The beer started to work on me. My lips numbed. Everything, the fire, the loudness, seemed far away, like I was behind glass. My head whirled, as if I'd spun around, around, like I used to do when I was ten.

Jonathan ran into the river, ran until the water covered his head. The riverbank was steep. We laughed. He bobbed in the water.

Then I remembered Jonathan couldn't swim. He struggled, sinking now, bobbed to the top, tried to touch bottom, sank again, bobbed up, down again.

Me and Mike looked at each other. Every year, almost, someone drowns in that river. Mike kicked off his sneakers. Mine weren't on. We dived into the freezing water. Jonathan glued on to my shirt. He almost drowned me. Somehow, Mike pinned his arms. Between us, we dragged Jonathan onto dry land. He stretched out by the fire, gasping like a fish out of water.

This might have sobered us up. But no. Instead, it started us all laughing, joking. Mike opened his beer. We stripped Jonathan down to his shorts, propped his clothes close to the fire. One of his socks fell onto the embers. It sizzled. The stink of burning rag stung my nose. Tom threw his vest over Jonathan's legs; Tony's went over his chest. Mike and me spread our vests out to dry.

After a bit, Jonathan stopped shivering and started snoring. The rest of us got louder, sillier. Finally, we ran out of steam and settled down by the fire.

Paul drank another beer. Vince stopped flying; he started pacing. Ted stayed the same right through the whole racket. It was like he looked in from the outside. Like he was there but he wasn't a part of it all.

By this time, my jeans were almost dry. Their stiffness rubbed my legs. I'd finished another beer and my head was spinning more than ever. I poked at the fire with a long stick. We huddled around the crackling blaze. The silver moon poked a curve through black clouds.

"I'm hungry," Paul grumbled. Other guys said things like, "Yeah, me, too."

Vince said, "Dad told me how his gang used to raid vegetable gardens, steal a hen, have a scoff. In the good old days."

"That was then." Paul sighed. "No one grows vegetables now. Or keeps hens."

"No, but..." Ted stopped until we all listened. "Naw. You guys are too straight. Never mind."

"Come on, Ted, tell us." Vince picked up another beer. He rubbed the bottle between his palms. Fast. Over and over.

"Picture it." Ted relaxed for the first time all night. He leaned against a long, fallen tree. The roots stuck in the air.

We all laughed. Ted was a pro at doing a takeoff on the old lady in *Golden Girls*.

"Picture it. Rows of red tomatoes. Fresh green lettuce. Carrots. Turnips. Turn a corner. Bottles and bottles of Pepsi, root beer, Orange Crush." He looked at Paul. "Bags and bags of chips. No live hens to pluck. But look, chickens! Plump. Juicy. Imagine them, roasting, over our fire."

Paul groaned. Vince licked his lips. Mike frowned. I closed my eyes, imagined food. My mouth watered. Ted's words poured over me. Into me.

He finished with "...and waiting, on the way out, are packs and packs of cigarettes, waiting. For you."

Ted's voice was liquid silver. I opened my eyes. Just a little. Moonlight stroked the water. Ted's voice fitted in with the dying fire, with the beat of Jonathan's snores. I felt like I was in a trance. Nothing could be better than to keep listening, listening to his words.

Ted lowered his voice. I wanted to hear him keep on talking...I closed my eyes. Lights danced behind my eyelids. Jonathan's snores stopped. I imagined him lying near me, warmed by the fire, almost naked, hypnotized, staring at the moon.

Ted whispered. I strained to hear his silver voice. "We can slip through a back window. Creep up the aisles. Borrow a cart. Have a shopping spree. No one will ever know. There's no harm in taking a little food. There's lots there. Lots."

"I'm starving," Paul moaned.

"You're always starving," said Mike. "Let's go home. It's getting late. I'll get wood for the next fire."

"There's so much food there." Ted's quiet voice made the sounds of the others ragged, useless. He talked, softly, smoothly. Everyone got quiet again. We listened.

I kept my eyes closed. Water splashed our shore with musical licks. I held onto the darkness, let the whirling fill my whole body.

Ted kept on talking. "We can go there." He kept coming back to that.

I wanted to stay right where I was. Not moving. Not speaking. Nothing before this minute counted. Nothing that would happen mattered. I knew Ted's words were dangerous. I didn't care.

"We can go there."

"Well, what are we waiting for?" Jonathan's voice boomed into the night, broke the spell. I opened my eyes, saw him leap quickly to his feet. He looked big and dark against the fire. I could see the muscles of his almost-naked body.

I sat up, shook my head. I should stop what was happening.

Jonathan tugged his damp sock over his big foot. "Where's my other one?"

"It burned." Vince tossed Jonathan his sneakers. The twins put on their vests. Mike and me put ours on. Jonathan dressed.

"The stores are closed." I buttoned my vest, tied my

sneakers. "We're not going there. We can't break the law, Ted."

Ted answered, "Jason, we've been breaking the law all night. Drinking underage. Doing drugs." He turned to Jonathan. "There's a window in the back of Food Central. Vince is small enough to crawl through. He can open the door."

"We can't do this. We'll get into trouble. Big trouble. We don't need this." I spoke to Joey. Maybe, he'd turn things. He could help me if he wanted. Joey stared at his fingers. "Joey, wake up. Tell them we can't do this."

"Look. At my fingers. At my hands. Geometry all over. Triangles. Everywhere." Joey smiled at me. "Pyramid power. Triangles can do anything."

He was totally spaced out.

"Come on, guys. Tom. Tony. Mike. We can't do this."

Mike looked at me. He drank his second beer. Straight down. "No one said *you* have to come along, Jason. It's a free country."

Tom said, "Jason, you never want to do anything. I'm in."

"Me, too," Tony agreed.

Elvis was on his feet. "I'm out of here. This is big time trouble. Who's coming with me?" He looked around our circle.

Joey glanced up from his fingers. "Not me. There's power here, can't you feel it?"

Mike took a step toward Elvis, stopped, sighed. "I gotta see it through."

Elvis turned to me. "Jason? How about you? You're not getting into this mess, are you?"

I looked around me. Jonathan pulled his laces tight. Paul picked up empty bottles, put them in the plastic bags. When we had enough, we'd trade them in on a dozen. Tom and Tony were doing a chorus dance, singing, "Hi-ho, Hi-ho, off to rob we go."

Vince kicked sand on the fire, killing its flame. Ted brushed sand off his clothes. Everyone was getting ready to move, to do something. I wanted to be with them.

Maybe, I'd stop them along the way. If I could. Maybe I'd just be there.

"Jason. This is crazy. Come on, man. Let's get out of here."

Elvis offered me a way out. If I went with him, Mike might come, too. If the three of us went, we might change the flow of the night, get the guys onto something else. That was the thing to do. That was the way to stop this mess.

When I sat up straight, everything around me went all wavy. If I stood up, I might fall. Ted looked down at me. If I went with Elvis, they'd all watch us leave. Ted would see me stagger; he'd laugh at me, at the way I couldn't hold my liquor. It was better to go with the crowd, link up with Tom and Tony, so he couldn't see I was unsteady.

All this took about five seconds.

"Well, are you coming?" Elvis asked.

"No. Go on. I'll catch you later."

He shrugged and walked away through the trees, all alone.

"Well, what are we waiting for?" Vince asked. "Let's go."

Jonathan echoed loudly, "Let's go."

Everyone turned to Ted. His eyes glowed red in the light of the last of the dying fire. He grinned. "It's all up to you. No one's forcing anyone." He rose to his feet.

I knew we were headed for trouble. I went with my gang anyway. I hooked up with Tom and Tony. I let myself be "easy-led."

CHAPTER FIVE

We were a noisy crowd. We paraded up the path, down Main Street, in behind Food Central. We didn't try to keep anyone from seeing us. Everyone, besides Mike and Ted, sang, "Hi-ho, Hi-ho, off to rob we go."

Cars drove past us. Music blared through the open door of the tavern. A bunch of guys stood outside; they laughed as we pushed past them. Ted faded into the middle of our pack. Jonathan marched up front. No one stopped us.

Soon, we stopped at the back door of Food Central. Everyone, even Jonathan, looked at Ted.

"Let's go home," I said. No one noticed me.

About two metres up, a small, open window led to a storage room. It had been a hot day. Staff must have forgotten to close it. Ted pointed to the window. "Ready and waiting."

Jonathan lifted Vince up on his shoulders, piggyback style. He moved in real close to the wall. Tom and Tony gave Vince a boost. Vince peeped inside, pushed the window up farther. With a final push from his helpers, he wriggled inside. We heard boxes tumbling. Vince cursed loudly.

"Keep quiet!" Jonathan roared. "Open up!"

"Give me a chance," Vince grumbled. He pushed open the door. The steel bar squeaked as the door opened.

Everyone, except Ted and me, rushed inside. "Scared?" he asked me.

I never answered. I pushed past him, followed my buddies. I felt like wiping that toothy grin off his face. Ted came in and closed the door.

It was spooky inside the store. The only light came from the fluorescents over the cooler and fruits and vegetables. The half-darkness made everything feel unreal, like a dream. Or a horror movie. I wandered around, watching everyone.

Paul sat in the aisle by the jumbo-sized bags of chips. He knocked down a mountain of silver foil, sat in the middle, ripped open three kinds of flavours. He leaned back against a shelf, looking as happy as if he'd just landed in heaven. He shovelled handfuls of chips into his mouth.

Jonathan grabbed Mike, tossed him into a grocery cart. Jonathan snatched a bunch of bananas, threw one to Mike, peeled one for himself. Mike tried to climb out of the cart. Jonathan shoved him down.

Tom built a pyramid of cans. He opened a can of Vienna sausages. He'd stack a can, eat a sausage, one at a time. When a six-can pyramid was built, Tony rolled a coconut down the aisle. It stopped short. He followed it with a melon. "I'm picking out the best bowling ball," he told me.

Joey ripped apart a pack of sliced ham. He sniffed a piece,

rolled it up, took one tiny bite. He held the ham tube up to his eye. As if it were a telescope. He aimed it at me. "Bingo! Got you!"

A shiver ran down my back. I turned to see whose footsteps followed me. Ted. We'd stopped by the tomatoes.

"Having fun?" he asked. He picked up a ripe, red tomato. Dug his fingers into it. Juice dribbled from the finger holes.

I strolled over a couple aisles to the cooler. Picked out a frozen coconut cream pie, ripped open the box, stuck a finger into the cool cream. It tasted nice, smooth and cool. Shivers crawled over me again. I turned. Ted aimed the ripe tomato at me. I smashed the pie at him, caught him bang on, ducked the tomato, and ran.

Ted caught up with me by the vegetables, hurled another tomato at me. He missed, grabbed a bunch of grapes. They fell apart when they hit me.

Jonathan tore up the aisle, straight toward us. Mike crouched in the cart. Jonathan ran over my foot. Ted squished another tomato, hurled it at me. I managed to get out of range. I glanced back. He slipped on the grapes.

I waited for him by the paper towels. When he got near, I ripped a pack open, threw it at him. The towels bounced and unrolled and unrolled. There's a lot of paper in one of those rolls. Ted picked up an end, wiped off his face.

"Now you're pretty," I jeered. I walked away, taking my time. Tom and Tony had moved on from the bowling lane. I speeded up when Ted got near. The cans tripped me and I rolled on a coconut. It split open, smeared my backside.

Paul yelled, "Watch it Jon! You're ruining good chips."

Up by the cash registers, Vince filled his pockets with

cigarettes. He shook a register. Dumb! There'd be no cash there tonight.

Ted stood over me. He juggled a can of corn on the cob, then aimed it at my head. He could kill me! I tried to get up but I tripped over cans.

That's when we heard the sirens.

CHAPTER SIX

Ted wiped the can off on his shirt, put it neatly on a shelf. He held his hand out to me. I took it. He seemed about to help me up. Instead, he bent my hand back and gave me a hard shove.

I fell back, hit my head on a can. Everything turned into black-lit, exploding flashes. When I could see again, Ted was gone. As I got to my feet, the bar on the back door squeaked. The door opened, closed, opened again.

Lights flashed on, made my eyes hurt. I ventured to the front of the store. Two cops stood by the light switch. They held Ted between them.

The younger cop took long strides toward me. He wasn't much older than me. He looked down the aisles. Torn chip bags, shattered coconut, tins everywhere, smashed cream pie, squished tomatoes, unrolled paper towels littered the floor.

"What a mess!" The policeman gripped my arm. He led me over to Ted and the older cop.

That man was big with reddish hair sticking out under his hat. Looked real mean. "Hands up against the wall!" he ordered. "Move it!"

I moved. The cop pushed Ted over by me.

Ted pointed at me. "It's his fault. Look what he did to me." He pointed to his face. The cream had dried; it pulled his face skin out of shape.

"That's nothing to what I'd like to do to you teenage vandals," the big guy growled. Ted shut up. He put his hands up against the wall.

The younger cop rounded up all the guys—Tom and Tony together and the rest, one by one. I counted. Seven. Vince ran past us, trying to get out through the door. The big cop picked him up by his collar. Vince hung there, his legs running like a cartoon character. He stumbled when the big guy dropped him.

"Resisting arrest, Mister?" The cop snarled.

"No, no, sir. Just looking for the bathroom," Vince squeaked.

"You'll have to wait."

Vince joined our line. Where was Jonathan? Breaking glass crashed and tinkled.

"Stay here," the big cop ordered. No one moved from the wall. I heard them pad toward the front of the store. By twisting a bit, I saw them go up opposite aisles. They had their guns out.

I shivered and shook all over. It was easy to believe Vince. I sure wanted to go to the bathroom. I looked down our line. Only Joey never looked white and scared. He stared at a odd-shaped stain on the wall. His hands were against the wall but he looked relaxed, like that's where he wanted them to be. "Looks like a tarantula," he said.

We all looked. He was right. So, who cared?

After a couple minutes, the cops returned. Jonathan was between them. Blood streamed from his right arm and the ankle of his sock-less foot.

"Stupid fool," said the younger guy. "Tried to escape through the window. All he had to do was open the door from the inside. He could have hurt himself on that glass."

"Too bad he didn't." Old red-hair sounded meaner, looked bigger every minute. He held Jonathan, who was quiet now, by the left arm. His partner went outside. He came back with a camera; he tossed his buddy a first-aid kit.

My arms ached. I wanted to take them down. The camera clicked pictures of our mess. Jonathan's cop took an antiseptic pad and wiped Jonathan's wounds. He pressed down to stop the bleeding and wrapped a bandage around the wounds.

Jonathan flushed. When the policeman finished, Jonathan mumbled, "Thanks."

Those big fingers had been gentle, I could see that. The cop just sighed and shook his head.

Tonight, those two were the only policemen on duty in our town. Real criminals might be getting away with murder, I thought suddenly. Then it came to me—tonight, we were the real criminals. My shivers and stomach cramps started all over.

"I'll come back for the rest," said the younger cop.

His partner nodded agreement. He added, "Tell the guard to keep an eye on that boy's cuts. Have a doctor check him before release. We don't want charges of negligence."

Jonathan, Ted and me were the first to go to jail. The police car shone under the bluish, parking lot lights. Paint chipped off under the front door. The licence plate started with GFE. Go free, I thought. I wish.

We were herded into the musty back seat, settled in on soft grey-blue fabric. When he slammed the door, I remembered a *Getting to Know Your Friends Day*. A policeman had told us the back doors of police cars never opened from the inside.

The officer opened the sliding glass between front and back seats. "Fasten your seat belts." He put on the siren, drove right through Main Street.

I wanted to cover my face. The whole world watched us, trying to figure out who was under arrest. I dreaded having to face my mom. I wriggled, bumped Jonathan's cut arm.

"Ouch!" he yelled, jerking away from me.

The ride was short. There was only one guard on duty. Henry Brown was the only other prisoner. He'd gotten drunk, had a fight, again. Henry almost lived in jail.

"We'll put those three in the cell with Henry," the cop (the guard called him Constable Hunt) decided. "There's six more to come." Constable Hunt shook his head. "Never saw anything like it. Likely to do anything."

He opened the barred door, herded us inside. "Usually, we let young offenders wait in a room, but I feel better having these guys in here."

He slammed the door shut. The bang echoed. The door locked automatically. They put Joey and Tony in with us; the rest of the guys went into the other cell. The cells were made for two people, but rubbing shoulders with my friends made me feel better. I rubbed my hands along the close-set bars.

Henry grinned down from his top bunk. He pointed to an opening. It looked like a mail slot. He had one yellow-grey tooth on his top gums and a Band-Aid on his chin. "They passes your meals in through there. So they don't have to open the door, so the jailbird can't punch the guard."

I didn't want to think about eating in there. Or using the steel toilet, right out in an open corner. It had no seat.

"Listen," Ted said. "Keep your mouths shut. Don't tell them anything. They can prove you were inside. Can't prove you opened the door." He didn't say "we."

Jonathan laughed too loudly. It wasn't a real laugh. "No. But they know I almost broke out."

One by one, they let us out to phone home. Ted made sense. I'd keep quiet until I saw a lawyer. They didn't ask for statements until our parents came. We all said we wanted to see a lawyer before we said anything. After we were released into our parents' custody, Constable Manuel, the big cop, ordered us to stay in town; he set times for us to make our statements.

The cops let me keep quiet. My mom didn't. She kept asking what was going on. I kept saying, "I'll explain later."

Finally, she said she'd come as soon as she could. "George is working the graveyard shift. I'll have to get a baby-sitter."

CHAPTER SEVEN

Before they let us go, a magistrate had to "remand" us. We had "committed an indictable offence." That didn't mean a thing to me.

Old Jack Cartier, the magistrate, came in wearing an apron with lobsters on it. Between forms, he grumbled. "I'm missing my family barbecue." He zipped through the paperwork.

I waited forever in that cell. I waited and waited for Mom while the other parents came.

Paul's mother swayed into the station first. All 300 pounds of her six-foot body, wrapped up in a bright, flowery dress about the size of a tent. "What have you horrible men done to my poor little boy?" she yelled. "I knows my Paul's not done anything bad. He's a good boy." She yanked tissues out of her huge, white, vinyl purse. When she rubbed her teary eyes, she smeared black stuff all over her face.

The guard let Paul out of the cell. The steel door clanged

shut. The sound went right through me, right down to my toes.

Paul's mother grabbed her son; she hauled him up against her big breasts. He almost smothered.

He wriggled away. "Aw, Mom. I'm okay."

"I know. Now that I'm here. You're going to be just fine." She grabbed him again.

"I'm hungry." Paul's muffled voice escaped.

She let him go. "We'll get a couple large fries on the way home." After the magistrate's paperwork, they left. She clutched Paul's arm.

Ted's parents came in next. His father was tall, stiff. His suit never had a wrinkle. He looked ready to lead a war meeting. Mrs. Dawson's black dress and two strands of pearls gave her a rich look. They say clothes make a man. Maybe.

The magistrate sure spoke nice to them. He even said, "I'm sure your son's not bad. Probably keeping the wrong company."

Ted's father nodded in agreement. "I'll straighten him out. He'll think twice before getting into trouble again."

Ted's mother kept quiet. Her face stayed real still.

CLANG! The cell door slammed again. Mom, hurry up!

Ted's mother moved toward him when he came out of the lock-up. His father took her arm, pulled her back. "We'll have none of your coddling tonight, Maria." He rubbed his belt grimly. "You've made him the way he is."

Ted flicked a look at that belt. He stepped back, looked at us in the cell. For a second, I thought he wanted to stay. He sighed and slumped his shoulders. Forms were signed. He left with his parents. All three of them walked far enough apart so they didn't touch.

Mike's mother, in her wrinkled, Kentucky Fried uniform, came in alone. She wiped her red, puffy eyes. You could tell she'd been crying hard. She answered questions in a thin, quivery voice. When the forms were done, she dared to ask, "Can we go now?" Then she started crying. Mike hugged her; he cried, too.

"I always thought you were the good one," she sobbed. "Lost hope for your brother years ago, Mike. Don't turn bad, too." Mike put his arms around her tiny shoulders as they walked out.

Each time the door opened, my heart skipped, hoping, fearing, it was my mom. What was I going to say to her?

The door opened again. In waltzed Tom and Tony's parents—their short, thin, dark-haired father and their ditzy, blonde mother. He took charge; she acted like a kid on a field trip. She brushed back her hair (messed up enough to be cute), blew a bubble, and looked around with wide, blue eyes. I wondered if her long, dark eyelashes were real. Only the tiny crinkles around her eyes and lips showed her age. She looked like she was a smoker. She'd know how to handle a cigarette so other women wanted to look like her.

"Wow, I've never been in a police station." She looked up at the big cop. "What have you done with my naughty boys?"

Constable Manuel took off his cap and apologized. "Sorry for your trouble, ma'am. Let's hope you won't have to come here again." He pulled out a chair for her to sit down.

The twin's father chimed in, "I hope not, either."

I wondered how those two had ever ended up together. While the twins' mother flirted with the cops, the magistrate, and the guard, her mousy husband filled out forms, answered questions. When the doors opened and Tom and Tony came out of their cells, they ran to their father. He took them each by an arm. They sailed out together. Their mother smiled and waved as they left.

What if my mom couldn't or wouldn't come? I didn't want to stay in there another minute. Jonathan stretched out on the lower bunk in our cell. Henry swung his feet from the top bunk. I held onto the steel bars, looked out, felt barred in—like a monkey in a cage.

Vince's father thundered in, smelling like beer. He stuck his thumbs in the front pockets of his faded blue jeans. He yelled at the cops. "Where's my boy? Picking on him, now, hey? Tired of locking me up, are you? Got to go for the rest of my family." He complained and swore through the usual routine, made the whole thing too long. It's a wonder they didn't lock him up.

Before they left (another slam of the door drummed through me), Vince's father grabbed Vince by the collar, bawled in his face. "Take me from a party again, and you'll be sorry." He let Vince go; then he seized his arm and dragged him away.

Vince told me once that his father either ignored him, beat him up, or treated him like a prince—sometimes all in one day. His mother just stayed out of his old man's way. His younger brothers were in a foster home.

Now only me, Jonathan and Joey were left. We'd been in there forever. My hands sweated. My head hurt.

"Want to change cells?" the guard asked. "Give you a place to sit."

I shook my head, no. For one thing, that would be like saying I'd be there longer. I didn't want to hear those doors banging any more than I had to. The sound hurt too much.

Joey's parents came before my mom. His father looked like he was in his late forties. His mother seemed too young to have a son going on eighteen. His father kept fixing his glasses, rubbing his head (he was one of these baldies who try to cover up by brushing a few strands of hair over the top) and complaining. He talked and talked.

Joey's mother, in black leotards and tiger-print top, wandered quietly over to the cells. Joey went up to the bars. He put his hands over two. She placed her hands on his. They looked at each other; neither of them said a word. She had the same hungry kind of gaze as her son.

His father grumbled, "We were having a lovely evening with friends. This had to happen. I insisted on finishing our meal. But we had to ask everyone to leave." No one listened as he talked on and on. They completed the routine.

"I'm sorry." Joey looked at me as the cell door opened.

"Don't sweat it. We were all in on it. All of us."

When he left, the bars seemed to get closer together. The cell shrunk. Mom still wasn't here. She might never be here. She might be too mad, too disappointed.

"Your parents aren't here yet, either," I said to Jonathan, just to stop the silence.

"They're not coming." He turned his face into the wall. His voice cracked a bit. "Old man said if I was fool enough to get myself into this, I deserved a night in jail. They were in bed."

"You're not in here for the night?"

"Looks that way." He took a deep breath. "I'll be okay."

I didn't know what to say. Every now and then, a tremor shook right through him. He didn't say anything else. His eyes were dry, but his body seemed stiff, tense. I sat on the bunk by Jonathan. They'd taken our sneakers and our belts. One of his feet was still naked, except for the bandages. I rubbed the cold, soft, smooth skin on top, the rough sole.

My mom was coming. It might take a while, but she'd be there. I knew that. I took off one of my socks, put it on Jonathan's bandaged foot. I tried not to hurt him too much. He winced a bit, but he didn't pull away.

He grinned at me. "You'll make a good nurse, Jason."

"Your foot's cold." I stayed there, sitting by his feet, neither of us talking. I was glad he was there with me.

The door opened. My mom came in. No one ever looked so good. She frowned at me through the bars, turned to the cop and got things rolling. She frowned while Constable Hunt pressed my fingers onto the ink pad and rolled them on the ID card. She watched while they snapped my picture, right side, left side, front on. I felt her hurting. She shouldn't have had to be there.

When we were finished, I looked back in at Jonathan. The cell door had clanged for the last time and he was still in there. All alone, except for Henry. He didn't count.

"Can I get an extra blanket for him?" I asked the guard. "He got wet earlier on; he might be getting a chill."

The guard opened a cupboard and passed me a scratchy, grey blanket. He opened the barred door and I tucked the blanket around Jonathan. "They'd probably let you go home with me and Mom, you know. I'll ask."

"No. That's okay. You go on. I'm tired. I'll be asleep in a

minute. My father will be here in the morning. You go on with your mother." He turned into the wall, closed his eyes. I patted his back and closed that barred door as softly as I could. I left with my mom.

I hated leaving Jonathan all alone in that cell, but I couldn't wait to get out of that place. I wanted to run to Mom's car.

She'd handled herself real well in the cop station. Looked normal, nice, dressed in dress pants and white blouse. She never said a word directly to me all the while we were inside. She saved it up for when we were alone.

CHAPTER EIGHT

"Hard to get a baby-sitter in the middle of the night. Didn't want to bother George." We piled into Mom's old, navy-blue Oldsmobile. She turned the ignition key, turned to me, spitting mad. She let go her drift, full force.

"Jason Allan Abbott! You should be ashamed of yourself!" The radio played *Don't Take Your Guns to Town*. She put the car in drive and took off, fast, zipped around the curves so fast and sharp that I swung from side to side. I almost went through the windshield when she stopped at intersections. "Couldn't believe my ears when the police called. First one in our family to have a chance to make something of himself and you're turning into a crook. You little fool. If the Rangers were in charge, you'd get a taste of the cat-o-nine tails."

"What's that?"

"Whip with nine stingers. Might do you good." She waited for traffic to pass by. Clubs were closing so there were a few cars on the road. She drummed her fingers on the steering wheel. "Well, what do you have to say?"

"Nothing, Mom. You're right. I'm stupid."

"Jason! You're not stupid. Ginny told me. This going to be a habit?"

"Mom! No. I'm not that dumb."

"Good. Glad to hear that. If you don't mean that, my son, you'll wish for the cat-o-nine tails."

Mom had only ever slapped me once when I was about eight. We had a big fight. Can't remember why. I jumped through my bedroom window, took off; she saw me, caught me, and right in front of the kids next door, she gave me a few good whacks on my backside. Having them watch felt worse than the smacks.

Even if she didn't smack, she had a way of making me feel I'd better listen. I might have been tough in school and on the outside. I was an angel at home.

She pulled into the All-Nighter, ordered me out. She worked there before she had Sherri. She was thinking about going back again. It was the only place in town still open. A few people sat around chatting. They were having a snack after the club. We sat in a dark booth in a back corner. No one else was near. Mom ordered coffee for herself, Pepsi for me and two coconut cream pie slices from Suzanne, the only waitress.

"I'm not trying to reward you. But I feels too cheap to take up space and only order coffee," Mom said when Suzanne left.

We ate first, kept quiet. Everyone else left. Mom ordered more coffee, another Pepsi. Little by little, she got me to tell her the whole story. I figured she might as well know the whole thing before she heard it all pushed out of shape on the gossip channel. I told her about the beer, the drugs, how we got caught up in a funny kind of mood listening to Ted.

She said one thing that I thought about a lot. She said drinking too much was the same as taking drugs. Still pushed my common sense out of the way. She said that was no excuse.

"See, I can understand your friends doing something that stupid. Paul, if there's a chance of eating, he's going to be there. Vince, that boy was born looking for trouble. Jonathan and the twins, they'll always go along with the biggest mouth. Mike don't know how to say no to the devil himself. I don't know this Ted Dawson, but he sounds like a real strife breeder all right—the kind that leads others on and keeps his own nose clean. Joey's got his head in the clouds more times than not. Half the time he don't know what side's up. So, it's no wonder they did what they did.

"But you, Jason Allan Abbot, you, who's been trying to show you're not stun, you sure acted stun. All along you knew what you was up to was wrong, didn't you?"

"Yes..."

"You knew and you went along anyway."

She sat up straight, looked down her nose at me, and gave me her ultimate put-down—the one she used when talking about fools. "Jason, my son, it's plain to see you let yourself be easy-led."

My ears burned. I gulped my Pepsi, looked down at my white paper place mat. I ran my fingers along the raised roses and leaves. It was hard to face her.

She kept quiet then. She waited until I felt small enough to crawl through one of the holes in the top of the salt shaker.

Chapter Nine

She backed off, took pity on me. "Ah, Jason, I s'pose it happens to the best of us. Back in the summer when I was fifteen, I was easy-led, too. Your dad was one sweet talker. Almost as good-looking as you. Five years older than me. He had a car. I fell stark raving mad in love with him. At least, I thought it was love."

She took a long, slow sip of her coffee, looked out on the dark parking lot. "I wanted to believe he loved me, too." She looked me straight in the eye. "Lousy, warm, teenage nights on the beach. Puts a spell on you, Jason. You forget who you are, what you believe in. Boy, in the middle of one of them nights, you gotta be some careful to keep your wits."

She went quiet for a couple minutes. It was hard but I kept quiet, hoped she'd go on.

"I had beer the first night. Wasn't used to it like it appears you are, you little sleveen. Moon shone. Water played music on the rocks. A little breeze ruffled the leaves. Hard to believe that anything outside that night meant a thing."

Mom hardly ever talked about her and my father. I wanted to hear more. I was almost afraid to breathe in case it'd make her stop talking.

"That night we became lovers. He led me up to it ever so gradual. Brought a blanket to the beach. Only natural to stretch out, look at the moon, make plans. Only natural to neck a bit. Touch a bit." She sighed. "Well, you can guess the rest."

A sign over the coffee pot said HELP YOURSELF. Suzanne was out of sight. Mom refilled her coffee, came back with a faraway look in her eyes. Almost like she'd forgot I was there.

"Funny how things changed after that. We didn't talk so much. Or touch. He had one thing on his mind. We started to fight. Foolish-like, I didn't get the Pill. We were always breaking up. So I figured I didn't need it."

She stirred coffee whitener into her coffee. "We even started seeing other people. The other guy I saw was nice to talk with. Couldn't kiss for beans. No danger of needing the Pill there, I tell you. Your father's new girlfriend, well, I could tell she was as crazy for him as I was. Got what he wanted, I'm sure. Left us both."

She gave another deep sigh. "S'pose it was just as well. If he'd married me, he would have blamed me for trapping him. I wouldn't want him feeling beholden to me."

She gave me a tired smile. "You look a lot like him. Smart like him, too. Hope you're nicer to girls, though."

"I don't have any girls."

"Good. Keep it that way."

"Well, I've gone out with a few. But none I liked a lot.

Have a better time with the guys."

"Hmph."

Suzanne peeped out from the kitchen. "Need anything?"
I shook my head, no. Mom told her, "Not now."

I was dying to go to the washroom, but I didn't want Mom
to stop talking. Mom chatted with Suzanne for a few minutes.
Then Suzanne disappeared again.

Mom took up her story. "March 1, 1976. Our last time
together. Incredible. He was leaving for the mainland,
looking for work. I knew, somehow, he wouldn't be back.
Not for me. He said he would. I didn't believe him. Not even
on that night."

She grinned, looked real young for a minute. "Those late
winter nights can be deadly, too. That's the night you got
started."

"Were you sorry?" I asked. I'd known I was an accident,
but not that she'd been on her own right from the first. What
would Mom have done if I hadn't come along?

"Yes. No. Well, boy, it's no picnic having a baby when
you're not much more than a baby yourself. If I'd had any
sense, I'da put you up for adoption. Times when I wonder if
I should have."

My heart turned to lead and sunk. So she hadn't wanted
me. She'd made a choice. Ruined her life.

Mom kept talking. "See, whenever you'd bring home a bad
report card, whenever I couldn't give you something you
wanted, whenever you'd get into trouble—like tonight—I
wonder if maybe you wouldn't have had a better life with
some richer, smarter couple. But Jason, once I saw you, it
would've broke my heart to part with you. I couldn't have

stood it. So, I couldn't give you up. You don't know what it did to me to see you locked up."

It's funny. This was the worst night of my life. And one of the best. But something wouldn't wait any more. "Mom," I said, "I've got to go."

"What? Where?" She was confused.

"I'm bursting. I got to go to the washroom."

We both started laughing. "I'll pay the bill." She left a tip and went to ring the bell at the cash register. I hurried to the men's room.

I just wanted to go home, go to sleep in my own bed. Tomorrow I'd face up to what I'd done.

Chapter Ten

"Get out of that bed. Now!"

I rolled over, looked at my clock radio—8:01 a.m. Too early to get up on a summer morning.

Mom pulled off my covers. "Do I have to bring in a bucket of cold water?"

"No." She'd be likely to do that if I pushed her.

Over breakfast, she told me she was getting a lawyer for me. "I'll pay for it out of an old life insurance policy I started for you when you was a baby. When I had hopes for you." She bit into her toast. "Still have a few hopes left, so I'm paying it back. Don't expect spending money until it's paid off." She drank her orange juice. "You're calling the manager at Food Central and apologizing. You're going there to clean up, too."

The toast stuck in my throat. "Mom. I don't want to do that." I tried to think of a way out. "It's saying I'm guilty."

"You are. You were caught red-handed."

I wasn't going there by myself. I called the other guys and, except for Ted, I talked them all into going along. Jonathan wasn't out of jail, yet.

We met in the front parking lot. Mom had called ahead. Jonathan had broken a huge, jagged hole in one of the bigger windows. It's a wonder he wasn't hurt more.

Mr. Grimm, Food Central's manager, rubbed his hands. He walked all around us. No one said anything. We looked mostly at our feet. Mr. Grimm gave us garbage bags, mops and buckets.

Paul started in on the grapes in a big way as soon as Mr. Grimm was out of sight. "Stop that, Paul!" I grabbed his hand.

Mr. Grimm came back, twitching his curled-up moustache, rubbing his hands. He said, "If you boys want a good word at the trial, you can put in a full day's work."

"Any chance of getting the charges dropped?" I asked.

"No, no. Not a chance. Company policy. Insurance. You know how it is."

I didn't, but I nodded. "I'll check with the guys." I called them all together.

"I was going to mow our lawn," Paul grumbled.

"How do we know the slink isn't just using us?" Vince asked.

We decided to put in the time. I called Mom. She said the police agreed to take our statements tomorrow.

Mr. Grimm didn't let us near the cash. I put Paul and Joey over with the Pampers, toilet paper and stuff. No food and nothing too interesting. I split up the twins and put Mike and

Tony on the vegetables, Tom and Vince on the meat. I mopped floors, kept an eye on them all.

Mr. Grimm calculated what he was saving in a notebook and smiled.

By ten in the morning, everyone in town knew what we'd done. People would come in, talk a bit, point at us. Then they'd point to the window. Some workmen replaced the broken glass.

My ears burned that day. Lunchtime I called Jonathan. He was out, finally. He came in with us for the afternoon.

Our court date was set: three weeks before school opened. A long time away. For the rest of the summer, we'd be in limbo. Tall, thin Ms. Robbins, my lawyer, never smiled at me once. Mom had heard from Suzanne who'd heard a bunch of lawyers talking when they had lunch at the All-Nighter, that she was supposed to be one of the best. So Mom wanted her and no one else.

Ms. Robbins said, "Get a summer job."

"Where?" I asked. "Who's going to hire me?"

"Find someone. Or, find somewhere to volunteer. Look like a model citizen who had a momentary lapse." She sounded like a teacher. "Since this is a first offence, you are unlikely to have to face closed custody."

Being locked up! That thought made my stomach cramp. She went on like her words were no big deal. "Find a job or volunteer. Prove you're a good kid."

She was right. If I had a chance of turning things around, it was now or never. People in town thought I was stun. Now they figured I was a crook. I hadn't been in a group since I quit Beavers. My only regular job was a long-ago newspaper route. My schoolwork was nothing to brag about. I didn't do up a resume.

At the Petrocan gas station, old man Curtis glared at me. "We don't hire criminals." He pushed in the cash register drawer and kept it closed.

Mrs. Simpson, of Simpson's Cash and Carry, crossed herself when I came in. "I only hire family members and young people in my church's youth group. Those who have good morals."

James Green ran a private campground. "I've got my staff for the summer." He leaned on his rake. "But if you've got some free time, you might give Nita Barrett a call. She's handling the Autumn Leaves Festival. You can draw, can't you?"

I called on Nita Barrett. She's a widow who's as broad as she's tall. She's an energy ball. Her kids are grown, living on the mainland.

"So you want to help. I'm always looking for helpers." She sized me up as I stood there on her doorstep. "Why? Who are you? I generally have to arm-twist young helpers."

"I'm Jason Abbott."

"Jason Abbott. Joan's son?"

"No. She's my nan."

"Then you're Marsha's baby. Yes, I can see you look just like your fa...mother's father."

She didn't fool me. She knew my father, knew I didn't. She kept talking, changed the subject so I was the one on the spot. "You got into trouble a few days ago." She nodded knowingly. "That's why you're here."

My face heated up. She had me bang on. "Come in, Jason.

Can you do carpenter work? Bake? Sing?"

"No. To all of the above."

"What can you do?"

"I can draw."

"Perfect. I need an artist. God works in mysterious ways."
She took a big pitcher out of her fridge. "Like iced tea?"

"Never tasted it."

"Well, take off that stupid baseball cap and have some."
She poured us two tall glasses, added shaved ice and lemon
juice.

It tasted strange, kind of nice. We sat at her kitchen table.
She cleared a space for our glasses. The table was piled with
travel brochures on Great Britain, a proposal for a grant for a
playground, an old Autumn Leaves Festival booklet and *War
and Peace*.

Nita told me about the Festival theme and the events
planned. I had to listen; she never gave me a chance to get a
word in edgewise. One thing was clear. She had her hooks
into me now. I wasn't about to get away without a no-pay
job.

Chapter Eleven

The next morning, I went to the Memorial High gym. Going into a school in the summertime was strange. Rain dribbled down my neck. It was pelting outside. I walked through the dark hallways, smelled the new wax. My footsteps echoed. It was too quiet. The gym floor was covered with blue plastic tarps, cans of paint, brushes. Rolls of brown paper, sheets of plywood, two-by-fours and a pile of tools took up a corner.

"Hello! Is anyone here?" My words bounced off the brick walls. A door by the side of the stage opened. Gareen Divine came through carrying a couple of white, plastic bags. I knew Gareen from school. She was a February baby. We were in the same grade. She'd missed the last part of grade four. A car accident kept her in the hospital for six months. They thought she'd die.

Gareen dropped her bags by the rolls of paper. She pushed her short, flame-red bangs back from her forehead. "Well,

well, what have we here?" She sized me up for about a full minute. I sized her up, too. She seemed to have more freckles than ever. Her glasses were as lopsided as always. "What are you doing here, Jason Abbott? Looking to steal a few cans of paint?"

That was Gareen all over. She put things on the line. That got them out of the way and we could go on from there. Nice and clean, with nothing cluttering up the space between us.

"Nita Barrett wants me to help."

"Trying to look good before you go to court, hey? Next, you'll go to Dad's church."

Gareen's father preaches at the Evangelical Revival. She must be a trial to him.

I got to know her a bit when we worked on a science project. She said her father had wanted a son. Six years after, daughter number three, Gareen, was born. Gareen's mother said she'd had enough of "being fruitful and multiplying." She'd had her tubes tied before she came home with Gareen. This made the pastor pretty mad. Too bad, said Mrs. Divine. Gareen was as close to a Garfield as they were ever going to have.

We eyed each other. "I didn't come here to be insulted." I pulled off my wet jacket. "I came to work. You get a chance to save my soul."

She laughed. "You'll have to see Dad about saving your soul. But there's plenty of work." She glanced around, picked up a battered, purple gym bag. She zipped it open and tossed me a towel. "You look like you need this."

"You must be a boy scout. Always prepared."

"I go to the beach in the evenings. Have a sandwich and a

swim." She looked over the mess around us. "It's quiet then. Everyone goes home besides me and the birds."

"So what do we do here?"

"'We shall design and paint the booths for the fair, the backdrops for the play, and anything else ordered by the mighty Nita Barrett."

"You can't draw." I knew that. We got an A in that science project. Mr. Bussey had paired us up. I had ideas. I found it hard to look up anything or to write it down. Once Gareen knew I wasn't just goofing off, she listened to me. She wrote down my words. I did the drawings. We got honourable mention in our school science fair.

"You can draw. You're here. Let's start."

We argued all morning. Between us, we came up with sketches for half a dozen of the projects and scrapped a dozen more. Other people dropped in and out. Gareen promised to give them all jobs.

You know the commercial where this guy says he noticed this girl for the first time after knowing her for years? It's his buddy's sister. Well, I found out what he meant that day.

Melissa Coldburn wandered in. I looked up from my sketches. I'd seen her around before, but I'd never really *seen* her. Like, she'd been just one more girl in the crowd. She held a tiny leather purse and spoke in a soft, tinkling voice. "I want to help. Nita sent me."

She looked down at me. My heart speeded up and a jolt quivered through me from my head to my gut. I couldn't stop staring at her. I went dumb.

Gareen came along, watched us with a tiny smile. She knew what was happening. Gareen spoke to Melissa. "I've seen your work on posters around school, Melissa. You've got a nice, light touch. You do the autumn roses for the play. Jason, you rough in the big picture, and Melissa, you fill in the details. Tomorrow afternoon okay, Jase?"

I nodded, yes. Not trusting my voice.

Melissa's gaze moved slowly from me to Gareen. She listened, nodded politely. "Tomorrow afternoon. I'll be here."

She walked to the door, stepping lightly, turned, stared straight at me (electric jolt again), waved, and left.

Melissa stands as tall as me. She's slender and moves with a flow, like a dancer. Her dark, soft, shiny hair swings around her shoulders and frames her rainy-day grey eyes. Her pale skin blushes just a bit, like the porcelain dolls George gives to my mom each Christmas.

Over the next two weeks, we worked together every day. Everything that I didn't do with Melissa was blurred. Everything I did with her stood out like 3-D. I saw, smelled, and felt everything more when she was near.

Gareen told us what she wanted. We argued. Then Melissa and I told our helpers what to do. We did the art work and they did the rougher work of big-scale, background colouring. For once, I was one of the people in charge. That felt good.

Gareen buzzed around giving out paints, pastels, chalks, brushes, nudging people who slacked off. One day, after we ate lunch, I did a quick sketch on a piece of scrap paper—a girl with long hair gazed from a high, castle tower. She had Melissa's face. A knight stood guard at the castle gate. This woman knight looked like Gareen. Gareen picked up the sketch and sighed. She passed it to Melissa. Melissa blushed and folded it into a small square. She put it in her little purse.

After the crowd left, if the day was still warm, the three of us would walk to the beach. There, I sketched Gareen's compact, full-breasted body; Melissa's long leanness. I drew them playing with a beach ball, rubbing sun screen on each other. I drew the smooth sweep of Gareen's arms as she swam, and the long, gentle curves of Melissa lying on her stomach, face turned to one side.

Sometimes, she'd undo the thin straps of her bikini top. "I don't want white lines," she'd say.

I'd hope she'd forget the ties when she turned, let the top fall. But she never did.

Sometimes, I dived into the cold water for a swim. The water covered something I didn't want them to see. Gareen might join me. Melissa never went in past her knees.

"I'll teach you how to swim," I offered. I imagined how it would feel to hold Melissa's body floating in the water.

"No. I don't like the water. It scares me."

I never touched either girl, never asked either of them out. I wanted to touch Melissa. Somehow, I wanted to touch her even more because Gareen was there. Gareen watched me watch Melissa. Except for Paul, Vince, and Ted, my other partners in crime gave in to my coaxing and helped a bit, too. Joey wasn't much good. He'd get sidetracked, spend an hour painting a few centimetres. Or he'd stop hammering and stare at the nail. He was high more times than not. I didn't know what to do about that. Most days, Joey sat on the grassy bank across from the tavern. He'd gaze at flowers or his hand or a rock. He hadn't changed, just gotten more spaced out than ever.

Our gang had sort of fallen apart. Ted, Vince and Paul hung around with a crowd that had a longer rap sheet than ours. They all wore studded leather jackets. Tom and Tony had met identical twin sisters. You couldn't pry them apart with a crowbar.

Elvis had been grilled good by the cops about his part; they checked his story with ours and finally gave him permission to leave town. He'd gone to the mainland with his brother. He hoped to hook a job. The rest of us weren't allowed to leave town before the trial.

Most of the time, the break-in seemed like something I'd dreamed. It was hard to believe we'd done that, or that our gang had been so close. Still, day and night, the same thought kept popping up, "What's going to happen to us in court?" That dark cloud just wouldn't go away.

CHAPTER TWELVE

I don't have to go to the gym. That was my first thought the morning after we'd packed it all away until just before the Festival started. What do I do now? We'd worked every weekday. I'd spent weekends with Mike, Jonathan or Joey. Twice, I went to the cabin with Mom, George, and Sherri. George never said much about my problem. He let Mom deal with it. We fished together on the cabin weekends. We still didn't talk much. We couldn't. We didn't know what to say.

That's the way it is with us. He treats me okay, but he's not my real father. That's in the way all the time.

Mom watched me more, now. When I left in the evenings, she'd ask, "Where are you going, Jason?"

"Out."

"Where?"

"Around."

"With who?"

"The guys."

"What's you going to do?"

"Don't know."

"Jason. Maybe you should stay home."

"Mom! Give it a rest. Leave me alone."

I hated the questions. When you're sixteen, plans ruin things. She threatened to ground me.

We worked out a deal. I'd say where I might be going, who I thought I'd meet. I promised to call if I was going to be late.

"Don't go drinking, Jason. Don't dare go drinking!"

I'd made up my mind to stay away from beer—at least until I was a lot older. I grumbled, but I said, okay. With her laying down the law, it was easier for me to say, *no*.

Anyway, now that the Festival work was done, I had to plan to see Melissa. I wanted to call her. Instead, I watched *Sesame Street* with Sherri. She used me for a "horsey."

She told me her two jokes. "Why did the fireman wear red suspenders? To get to the other side! Why did the chicken cross the road? To keep his pants up!"

After lunch, I walked past Melissa's house three times. A curtain moved. I went home and paced. I was getting worse than Vince.

"What's wrong with you?" Mom asked as she peeled potatoes. "You got the worms?"

"Got nothing to do."

"I got lots for you to do. Put a load of light in the washer. Bring up the load in the dryer."

After supper, I picked up the receiver and dialled the first three numbers three times. I'd memorized her number weeks ago.

I flipped through an old hockey magazine. Then I noticed I was holding it upside down.

Melissa my mind sang, over and over. I drew her hands on my sketch pad, small, pretty, spattered with paint. She smelled like a rose. I imagined feeling her body cuddled up to mine.

At nine o'clock, I went to the bathroom, combed my hair, and ordered the face in the mirror to *DO IT NOW!*

My sweaty hand stuck to the receiver.

Melissa answered. "Hello? Who's there?"

I managed to say, "Hello." My voice cracked. I cleared my throat. "Hi. This is Jason Abbott."

"Jason. I was thinking about you all day."

I knew it. Now, all I had to do was ask her out. We talked about nothing for the next hour.

"I have to go. Mom's giving me funny looks." She giggled. "See you later."

"Wait, Melissa...how about meeting me at the beach tomorrow. If it's sunny."

"Sorry. I'm shopping with Mom."

My heart sank down past my navel, down past my toes. "Oh. Well. That's okay."

"How about Wednesday night? A movie?"

I had no money for a movie. Still, I had two days. Maybe I could mow a lawn or something.

"Perfect. I'll pick you up at seven."

She was quiet. I held my breath. "Jason? I'll meet you at the corner of Main and Fifth. It'll be better that way."

"Sure. If that's what you want. The corner of Main and Fifth at seven o'clock. Wednesday." I wanted to be sure we both got it right.

I kept waking up all night. The next day, I knocked on the door of every senior around. Old Mrs. Brown sent me to pick up her groceries. "Make sure you get the specials," she ordered. I mowed Jack Howe's lawn. Luckily, he didn't notice I cut down a tree he'd planted. Mrs. Pickering, who's got arthritis, paid me to pick her own strawberries. I made thirty dollars.

I got to the corner half an hour early. Melissa got there half an hour late. My feet were wore raw from pacing. You can see my tracks in the sidewalk.

I don't know what the movie was about. Melissa giggled a lot. I put my arm around her shoulders. She nestled against me like a soft, silky kitten.

As soon as the curtain closed, she looked at her watch. "Oh! Look at the time. I've got to be home by eleven. We'd better hurry." She stopped me at the last intersection before she turned off to her street. "This is far enough."

"I want to walk you all the way home."

She smiled at me, squeezed my hand. I kissed her hand, then put it around my neck and held her close. When we kissed, her lips were softer than I expected. They drew me in, made me want her, made me want to take care of her, forever. We kissed under a street light, under thousands of fluttering moths trying to kill themselves on the glass. A car zoomed by, honked at us. I looked up, dazed. Across the street, a curtain closed quickly. The kissing left me feeling confused, almost like I didn't quite know where I was.

Melissa gave me one more quick kiss. "I got to go. Jason, don't walk down my street with me. Please."

I shrugged. "I'll watch you from the corner. See that you get home okay."

She ran down the sidewalk. Her feet hardly touched the ground. I floated home.

We saw each other every chance we got for the next week and a half. I never walked her all the way home. She said, "Mom says you're a bad influence. She had a fit because we worked together. She'd die if she knew I was seeing you."

"I don't want to make trouble for you."

She kissed me again and I figured we'd handle any trouble together. On sunny beach afternoons, Melissa played her tapes—Meat Loaf, Pink Floyd, Bare Naked Ladies. She'd chat with her girlfriends, ignore me. At night, under our favorite street light, she'd let me kiss her like I'd never kissed another girl. She smacked my wandering hands away from her more interesting parts.

In the late afternoon, I'd go home, grab a sandwich, go back to the beach. Gareen was usually there. We chatted and argued about everything from school to the value of the space program. Then I'd go meet Melissa.

When I talked about Melissa, Gareen kept quiet. I never told Melissa about my chats with Gareen. Melissa chattered, I listened. Lots of times, I wondered how to get close to her mother. I'd wonder if I'd be locked up. Melissa never noticed if my mind was far away. She never noticed I was scared.

One evening, Charlotte, a cousin of Gareen's joined us. Charlotte was taller than me. She was really stacked. She was strong, too. She exercised and worked out with weights. She'd worked in some kind of gym on the mainland, along with her father, for years. When she flexed her muscles, she made every single one stand out sharply. Then she'd let them all go normal, and she'd look better than other girls.

When Jonathan met Charlotte, she did a few demonstrations. When she flexed her muscles, Jonathan fell head-over-heels in love. They kept looking at each other like lovesick cows.

When Jonathan went for ice cream, Charlotte watched him leave, waiting for him to come back. "A lot of guys are scared stiff of a strong girl," she said. "Dad's thinking of setting up a fitness centre here in town. We'll move back here then."

Jonathan's parents didn't want him to get a lawyer. They said he should "pay" for what he'd done. All the rest of us had a lawyer—either a paid one or one from Legal Aid. He could have gotten one on his own, but he wouldn't go against his parents. Our court date was Thursday. I was scared for him. Scared for all of us.

Chapter Thirteen

I called Melissa on Wednesday morning.

"Gee, I'm sorry Jason. Can't see you today. This big family dinner is on for tonight. Mom's sister and her brood rolled in from Nebraska."

"But Melissa—"

"I want to see you. I just can't. Okay?"

I swallowed hard. "Tonight? After dinner?"

"Auntie's showing slides. I can't skip off."

"I might be locked up tomorrow night."

"Yeah." She was quiet. Her voice went real low. "I'm sorry, Jason. I'll think about you. But I can't see you today. Or tomorrow." Her voice went lower. "Mom found out. She said she'd get a restraining order if you hang around me."

I went all cold. I imagined Melissa twirling her hair, being careful so no one heard her. Acting like I was a dirty secret.

"I don't want to cause any trouble. Don't worry, Melissa. I won't bother you again."

I slammed the receiver down. For a long time, I shivered. My throat hurt and my eyes stung. I washed my face with cold water and took a few long, deep breaths before I went downstairs.

Mom and Sherri were at the hairdresser's. Mom gets her hair done when she's worried. I hoped she wouldn't hear anything bad about me there.

I decided to go across town to see Nan. I'd lived there until I was ten. In a way, I feel more at home there than I do in George's house. Nan was folding towels when I walked in. She dropped the bath towel in her hands, waddled over and grabbed me in a bear hug. I sunk right into her warm floppiness. The coldness left me.

"Jason, my son, I'm some scared. I'll put the kettle on." Two of my uncles are younger than me. They weren't home.

A toilet flushed. Pop came out of the bathroom, buckling his belt. "Hello, boy. Still getting into trouble?" He always said that.

"Stop that, Hedley! Jason's not bad." She always said that. Nan sliced off homemade bread. She put partridgeberry jam in a bowl and opened a can of cream. That's my favorite treat. My mom doesn't make much homemade bread and jam.

Pop turned off the kettle and plunked into a chair by the table. He didn't know what to say. He leaned forward a bit, took his wallet from his back pocket, gave me a ten-dollar bill. "Take it, go on," he insisted when I pretended I didn't want it. Before long, I got itchy feet and left.

After court, I mightn't be able to go where I wanted. Even now, Melissa was off limits. The weather kept changing. I shivered in my T-shirt. Black clouds gathered in the hills.

I thought about Gareen. She probably wouldn't want to see a criminal either. I was a marked man. My stomach growled. Lunchtime. I wandered home.

Mom made me a ham sandwich and chicken noodle soup. She was too quiet. She snapped at Sherri. That's strange for her. The worry crease in her forehead was real deep today. The phone rang just as I finished my soup. Me and Mom jumped.

"Jason?" It was Gareen. "How are you doing? I've been thinking about you all morning."

I sat on the sofa, stretched the tangled cord. "Thanks. I've been thinking of you, too."

"Really? You're not with Melissa?"

"Naw. Her mother heard about us. Got pretty upset. Guess it's over between us." I tried to sound like I didn't care.

Gareen was on to me. "That's too bad. Go for a Coke?"

"Sure. Meet you at the Take-Out."

Mom had listened. "Here." She handed me a fiver. "I know you can't sit still today."

Gareen and I sat in the Take-Out most of the afternoon. While we talked, I drew pictures of barred windows on napkins.

She picked one up. "You're scared."

"Yeah." I didn't want to say anything else. She took my hand, pressed it for a minute. It was four o'clock and we were still on our second Coke. Supper customers were trickling in. The counter man glared at us; we decided to go home.

"Thanks, Gareen." I stopped by her gate.

She grinned. "I had nothing else to do."

She slapped my back. "It'll work out. It's your first offence.

Won't be too bad. Call me and let me know what happens."

Later, I found out her church was hosting a revival meeting for groups from all over the province on that Thursday. I heard that Reverend Divine was pretty mad when Gareen disappeared for the whole afternoon. Gareen never mentioned that.

Joey called me after supper. We'd hardly been together since the break-in. He sounded excited, like he was waiting for something good. "Let's get together tonight, Jason, all of us."

"Yes. I'll call Mike, Jonathan, the twins."

"I'll call the rest. We'll meet at the turnaround at the end of Main Street."

When we met at seven, thunderclouds made the sky dark. The coming storm weighed the air down, made it still and waiting. My vest felt like an old friend. The others, besides Paul and Vince in their studded, leather jackets, wore their vests, too. Ted didn't come. That was fine with me.

They say the criminal always goes back to the scene of the crime. I guess it helps him remember how it came about. Jonathan headed down our trail. We all followed. The alder leaves, drying out already, crackled as we pushed through. I picked a few raspberries and threw away the ones with rotten kernels or white grubs. The rest tasted sweet and gritty.

We came to our blackened fire pit in the middle of dull, tan-coloured sand. Black water rippled through the still, heavy air. Our hideaway was bleak in the thundery evening.

"Let's light a fire." Tony spoke quietly.

"Naw. It's going to rain. Can't you feel it?" As soon as Tom said the words, the rain started. Huge drops bounced on my bare arms, soaked through my vest in minutes. We ran under the trees. Rain danced down through the leaves, peppered the black water. Thunderclaps boomed right over us. The ground shook. Lightning flashed in front of us.

"We'd better get away from the trees. Get out in the open." Mike was being sensible.

No one moved. We dared the lightning.

"Take off those metal studs," Joey warned Vince and Paul. He unzipped their jackets.

"Hey," Vince yelled, "get your hands off me."

Joey took off Vince's coat; Paul passed him his. Joey tossed the jackets toward the water. The arm of one dragged in the river. Vince took a step toward his coat. Lighting flashed, danced along the studs, tripped merrily right into the water, casting chain-like flashes on the river.

"Awesome!" Joey's eyes glowed. He looked totally, absolutely alive. He looked at us. "Metal buttons on our vests and jeans."

We stripped, threw our vests and jeans atop the jackets. We stayed huddled together, knew we shouldn't, watched the lightning flash all around us, tingle right inside our skins. It tossed off a smell of ozone and thunder. We felt all together, part of a whole, stronger because of the others. The thunder claps rumbled and we cheered.

Gang feeling. It was easy right then to remember how we'd ended up at Food Central. A strong guy can grab into a mood, spread it like a germ, quick, to the whole crowd. Ted could do that. So could Joey.

Joey gathered us in with his excitement. We crowded, almost naked, around him, watched the storm build up, fade away. Ten beats after the thunder the flashes flared—the show was over. We were wet and shivery. We shook sand out of jeans and vests, sorted out who owned what.

Paul said, "I'm hungry."

"Well," answered Tony, "let's not go to Food Central." Everyone laughed, a bit sadly.

"Let's go to the All-Nighter," said Vince. Tom and Tony went to see their girls. Charlotte was flying in from the mainland in the morning.

Everyone was quiet at the All-Nighter. We ate quickly and went home. Our wet, sandy clothes stuck to us, made us feel gritty. Thoughts of the next day hung over us. I was home by eleven.

Mom looked up from her cross-stitch pattern. "Good. You're home. You look like a drowned rat. Get a good, hot shower and some rest."

I listened, figuring I wouldn't sleep a wink. But I didn't wake up until six o'clock. Summer sunshine poked through my blinds; it made barred patterns on my bedroom wall.

CHAPTER FOURTEEN

irds chirped. Warm, fresh air drifted in through my window. I always left it open a bit on summer nights. Did cell windows open at all? It was going to be a perfect, late-summer beach day. I put my pillow over my face.

It was no use. I couldn't forget or get back to sleep. My clock radio dial switched numbers to read 6:04. Almost three hours of freedom left. I punched my pillow, stretched a few times, crawled out of bed.

While I dried off, after my shower, I checked to see if I needed a shave. The guys called me "Baby Face." They'd all been shaving for years. I could see a bit of a black shadow over my top lip. I looked at George's razor. No, the shadow didn't look scruffy. It made me look...mature.

"Dress neatly. Look respectable. Watch your manners." Those were orders from Ms. Robbins.

Mom had bought me a new sports jacket and pants, shirt and tie. I hated dressing up. It made me feel all tight and cramped. My old dressy clothes (bought for Sherri's christening) were way too small.

Yesterday, George had fixed my tie. He was working out of town for the day. I was careful not to untie the knot. I might never get it tied again.

I had a fast breakfast of instant oatmeal, toast, and orange juice. Then there were three trips to the toilet. I was nervous.

Finally, we were on our way. Mom dropped Sherri off at Nan's. I was glad Sherri was too young to know what was happening. Nan hugged me and cried.

"I hate this." Mom drove real slow. "It's the second time I've been to court for you."

"No, it's not."

"Yes it is. See, like I told you, your father was long gone before I even knew I was pregnant. Mom and Dad weren't too flush, not too much work, a crowd still home. Social worker said I should try for support from your father, or at least put in a claim saying you were his. In case I needed help later on." She stopped at a stop sign.

"I didn't want his help, but maybe if I'd talked to him first, he'd have kept in touch with you."

The traffic let up and she turned right. "I was just a kid...thought the grown-ups, especially this woman in a nice suit, knew best." Mom was quiet for a minute. "I told you I was seeing someone else besides your father. Seeing this guy, talking to him, that's about it. Well, your father's mother said I was trying to trick her son. She demanded a blood test. She said that in court, made me sound like a tramp. I started bawling, took off from that court room and never asked them for nothing after."

Mom stopped at another sign. She looked at me, nodded her head. "When she sees you now, she knows you're his, blood test or no. You're the spitting image of him."

So. I had another grandmother in town. "What about...my father? Is he still around here? Does he come home?"

"He's got a real good job in Fort McMurray. Comes home sometimes in the summer. Leave it, Jason. He's got his own family. No need stirring up old messes. We're doing okay without him."

I kept quiet. I'd watch for a man who looked like me. Some woman Nan's age might size me up more than normal. My friends wouldn't tell me who they were—unless I asked.

I stared at the Community Hall. Court was about to start. I wanted to stay in my mom's safe car. All four doors opened from the inside. The cars of the other guys' parents were already there. Ted's father's Lincoln was missing. That was odd. Dr. Dawson seemed the type to be early.

"Come on. It's getting late." Mom held her door open, frowned at me. We went in together.

CHAPTER FIFTEEN

That morning in the Community Hall, where they hold preteen dances, bingo and court once a week, is blurred. The smell of stale smoke (from bingo the night before) hit me when Mom opened the door. Rows of cheap, wooden chairs (like the ones in Bill's cooler) were set up in front of a longer table. The magistrate, in a long, black robe, peered at us over his bifocals; he stood at a stand with a slanted top and a microphone. He kept testing the microphone while we found chairs in the back row. His voice scratched on my nerves. The lawyers sat on the side. We had to sit by them during the trial.

Our lawyers had asked for a closed court because, except for Jonathan who'd turned eighteen last week, we were all juveniles. He'd been seventeen at the time of the break-in so he was being tried with us. Mom whispered to Mike's mother. She said Ted was having a separate trial.

Jonathan looked good. I'd talked to him about that. His parents weren't rich, but they weren't hurting for a dollar. His father, who was big, husky, always scowling, owned a construction company. His tall, thin mother dressed nice; since I'd been hanging around with Jonathan, I'd never seen her smile much or say much. Jonathan's not one to complain, but I know he's never gotten a whole lot of attention, even though he's an only child. He said once that he felt like a boarder they didn't really want. We never hung out at his house.

"Pre-disposition reports" had been made up for each of us. We were all first-timers. To make up this report the cops had talked to each of us, our parents, people we'd worked with or for, and our teachers. They'd checked school records. It was like being stripped naked. The court knew more about us now than our own parents did. My lawyer told me this and I told my buddies. They got a few good words put in after I pushed them a bit. Their lawyers hadn't said anything about "character witnesses." Joey's drama teacher said, "The boy has potential. He totally gets into the feel of his character." Drama was an easy credit. A neighbor of Tom and Tony said, "They're wonderful baby-sitters. My children love them."

Paul and Vince called an old Sunday school teacher. She said, "They're active, but good, boys."

I'd had a good school year compared to my past. Nita Barrett had praised me for my work with the Festival. After a nice bit of my sweet-talking, and a few exaggerations about how much my friends had helped, she said a few good words about them, too. The magistrate had looked over all this stuff before the trial.

The police gave their own and the statements of witnesses. Some of the guys from outside the tavern had said they'd seen us going up Main Street, singing all the way. A woman near Food Central saw us going toward the building.

Mr. Grimm told of the damage. My lawyer also got him to tell how we'd "done an excellent job cleaning up. Volunteered. Did a fine day's work." He added, "Mr. Thomas, father of Jonathan Thomas, replaced the window. No cost to the store."

That was news to me. Jonathan looked surprised, too.

I felt like I was on another planet, watching. Like none of this was real. Funny the things I noticed, the things that stick in my mind: how the room got hotter and hotter; the cool blast of air when someone opened a window; the way a sunbeam lit up the row where Jonathan's and Paul's parents sat. Little flakes of dandruff dusted Paul's plaid jacket. Jonathan's father's hair was slightly greasy. Joey leaned forward, reached out his hand to touch the dancing dust of a sun ray.

We were each called to the long table to testify. We were only allowed to answer questions. No one asked us how it really happened. We all came out looking bad. Jonathan looked the worst.

"When all of you left the beach, who went first?"

"Jonathan, but—"

"How did Vince gain access?"

"He climbed on Jonathan's shoulders, but—"

"Thank you."

That's the way it went. They twisted the way it was. They made it look like we were innocents led astray by this big, older guy. It helped that we all had lawyers and Jonathan didn't.

They could prove what we did—even if we had pleaded not guilty. We'd been caught red-handed. There were witnesses and our own statements. They got it all wrong. They wouldn't let us explain. Not even our lawyers. Especially not our lawyers. They wanted to get us off with the lightest rap possible. That's what this trial was about.

No one asked questions about Ted. He wasn't even called as a witness. Guess they didn't need him. I wondered how he'd managed to get his own trial.

The room got stuffier. Sweat soaked my dress shirt. I was glad I'd put on deodorant. I could smell someone who didn't. The heat made the smoky stink worse. Awful room. Like hell.

Except for a half-hour lunch break at Kentucky Fried, we were stuck in there from nine until three-thirty. At least, I thought, we'll know where we stand now.

Instead, the magistrate took off his bifocals, cleaned them, and ordered us back next week, same time, same place for sentencing. The magistrate asked us each if we had anything to say for ourselves about why we'd gotten involved in this "incident."

Vince said, "We were drunk. And we were stoned. And there was nothing else to do."

Paul said, "We were hungry."

Tom said, "It seemed like a good idea at the time."

Tony said, "We never meant to hurt anything or anybody."

Joey said, "No comment."

Mike said, "It was all my fault."

"Oh?" The magistrate frowned at him. "Explain, please."

Mike looked at his mother. Tears rolled down her cheeks. His lawyer shook her head, no. Mike said, "I mean, I should have tried to stop it. Jason tried."

I was next. Dry throat. Tongue stuck to the roof of my mouth. Sweaty palms. "It was dumb. I should've left with Elvis. Should have talked the guys out of it. None of us did that kind of thing before. We won't again, either."

The magistrate said, "Hmmpf! If I had a dollar for every criminal who promised not to stand before me again, I'd retire. Your sentiments are worthless."

Jonathan was next. He was beet-red, glistening with sweat. "Can't explain it, sir. Seemed like something we all wanted to do. It just happened. Don't know why." He looked at me. "Like Jason, I promise we won't do anything like that again."

The magistrate didn't bother to answer with more than another "Hmmpf!"

There we were. Left hanging for another week.

Chapter Sixteen

It was a crazy week. I couldn't resist. I called Melissa. "Wait a minute. I'll talk to you in my room." She hung up; before she picked up the phone again, I heard a little click.

Melissa didn't give me a chance to say another word. "Listen, I can't see you tonight. Family stuff. Meet you at The Park tomorrow. Around one." Then she hung up.

The Park is a small circle of raggedy grass with three roofed picnic tables and a big, old birch right in the middle. They're talking about chopping the birch down before it falls on power wires, or a car, in one of our windstorms.

I was in The Park by twelve-thirty the next day. By one-thirty, I had a path scuffed through the grass. I carved out my initials on a picnic table. I had a pocket knife, but I would have done that with my fingernails just to pass the time! She wasn't coming. She hated me. She was in an accident, because she'd been hurrying to see me. She's barred in, grounded.

Forever. I went from hating her to loving her a thousand times in that hour. I worried about her. I wanted to shake her or kiss her. I decided to wait until two and then leave. I might have waited forever.

At 1:46, according to my digital watch, Melissa strolled up the street, taking her time. She was with two other girls. I wanted Melissa to myself. They stopped at the broken gate.

"I'll meet you at the Take-Out. I won't be long," she told her friends. One of the girls, Doreen Mercer, smiled at me; the other stared at me like I was an animal in a zoo. She giggled.

Doreen said, "Come on, Sue. Let's give them some time alone." She took Sue by the arm. They walked on down the road.

Melissa stood at the gate for a minute or more. I sat on a picnic table. We stared at each other, not saying anything. The hunger started beating through me just like always. I forgot she was late. It didn't matter that she hadn't been there when I needed her. I just wanted to hold her next to me.

She ran to me, like she felt the same tugging feeling. I slid off the table and opened my arms. She melted against me like she never had a bone in her body. A car hummed toward us. Melissa stepped away from me. Her grey eyes were almost black. Her lips trembled.

"I can't see you any more, Jason."

"I know."

"It's not fair." She turned away from me, started toward the gate, changed her mind and sat on a picnic table, swung her feet. I stood in front of her. She turned her head away. "Miriam Keeping reported on our necking. She lives across from our street light. Mom's seriously mad. Says I'll ruin my reputation hanging around with you."

"What do you think?"

"Jason, you're not like she thinks, but I don't want to be grounded for the last few weeks of summer. Besides, I don't like fighting. And I don't want to get you in trouble."

I stuck my hands in my pockets. Looked up at the blue sky. "I don't want to get you in trouble either."

Her voice was soft, sad. She sat there looking at me with a lost Bambi look. "You can always go out with Gareen."

"Don't you care? I'd care if you went out with another guy."

"Well, I care. But, like, she's a nice girl and she's my friend, sort of, and if you go out with her, I'll still see you sometimes. And like, then my parents won't hassle us."

"That's using her."

"She won't mind. She likes you."

"We're friends. I wouldn't do that to her. If I took Gareen out, it would be over between us."

"Well, like, maybe that's the way it's gotta be."

"So, you don't really care about me at all."

"I never said that."

"You pretty well did." I gave it one more try. I asked, "What if you introduced me to your folks, let them get to know me, see that I'm not the Big Bad Wolf."

"No way, Hosea. You don't know my mom. She's got a one-track mind." She patted the picnic table and I sat by her. "Mom and Dad aren't bad. I get almost everything I want. I listen to them, stay out of trouble. Everyone's happy." She held my hand in the softness of hers. "I never wanted to go against them before I met you. It's been hard, seeing you this long. Honest."

We walked to the tree, sat on the grass, leaned against the white trunk, stayed quiet. The grass had been cut that morning. Its fresh-cut smell made me feel like I'd lost something forever. Sunlight poked light patches through the leaves. Melissa leaned against my shoulder like she belonged there.

She'd just torn up my insides. Now she acted like nothing had changed between us. Should I let her sit there relaxing against me? Should I tell her to get lost? I let her sit there. She could have sat there beside me forever. I wouldn't have said a word.

Melissa picked up a handful of cut grass, tossed it to the ground. "Oooh!" She leapt to her feet, yanked me up, too. "Look, red ants! They bite!" Dozens of ants crawled through the scraggly grass. I started to itch. We brushed each other off, checking for ants. I forgot the ants and brushed her where she'd never let me touch her before. She laughed, shoved me away. I kissed her, softly.

She let herself go soft against me for a single second. She moved away from me slowly, turned so I couldn't see her face. She took a deep breath. "I'm sorry, Jason. It's not up to me."

It is, I thought, it is. You could let me try to talk to your mother at least. I knew Melissa was soft, in every way. That's why I felt stronger around her.

"Before you go," I flicked open my pocket knife, "let's do one thing for old times sake."

"You don't want to make us blood brothers or anything, do you? Or make vows? I'm not into stuff like that."

I laughed. "Me neither. No. Let's carve our initials into this old tree."

She watched while I pulled away a patch of bark and carved a heart. *J.A.* + ... I handed her the pocket knife.

"Watch for ants," she ordered. She was slower than me. Added a curve to her letters. *J.A.* + *M.C.*

After I'd closed the knife, she let me hug her until we heard another car coming. Her scent of roses, her rose petal skin, the late summer sounds, all wrapped around me. I'll always remember Melissa in my arms.

She stepped apart from me before the car came too close, rubbed the corners of her damp eyes, careful not to smear her mascara. "I have to go. See you around, Jason."

"See you around, Melissa."

She stopped at the broken gate. "Don't call me. Please."

I watched her walk down the road, straight and slim, head up, not looking back. She could have ended it easier with the old line, "Don't call me, I'll call you." We could have laughed.

I felt totally numb. I called Gareen that night. She probably knew the whole story, but she let me tell her about court, let me tell her about Melissa. "I don't feel anything. I don't understand it," I said.

"You're shell-shocked. Too much coming at you at once."

She was right. The next morning, I started hurting. I wanted time to fly. I wanted time to stand still. I was sick of this limbo. I stayed home, drove Mom crazy, made Sherri happy. Sherri followed me around like a little puppy. I took her to the library. She made me read the *Fuzzy Yellow Duckling* ten times. I tried reading other books. The words were all tangled up.

I was broke and too keyed up to find an odd job. I saw the guys a few times. All of us, except Ted, were coming together for this week. Ted's trial hadn't started. He was pleading "Not Guilty." He'd appear before a judge and jury.

Joey stayed clean. He kept us all up with him on a curious artificial high. We gathered around him. He didn't seem scared.

Jonathan, Tom and Tony spent most of their time with their girls. I chatted with Gareen every day. I didn't ask her out. It wouldn't have been fair. It wouldn't have made sense.

Most of the time, I felt like I was in my own little box and I didn't want to let anyone else in, not even Gareen, to really share the darkness. Melissa never called.

"You're either lovesick, or you're using the idea that you are to keep yourself from thinking about the sentencing." Gareen was playing shrink and counsellor. We sat on a bench in The Park. Somehow religion came up. I'd gone to church with Mom when I was little. Never got a thing out of it. "I don't even know if there is a God." I waited to see what she'd say.

"Oh, there's a God."

"You sound awful sure."

"Yes. I don't know all about this God. Don't think anyone does. Not even Dad."

"But you believe there's something."

"Yes. Let's try something. Close your eyes."

I obeyed, trusting her.

"Keep quiet. Real quiet. Listen. Not to me, to the world around us, let your mind go blank."

"You sound like Kung Fu."

"Okay. Don't try it. Don't tune in." She sounded miffed.

"Sorry. Give me a minute." I tried to force myself to stop thinking.

"Don't try too hard."

"I follow you, Master."

It took a while, but all at once I knew what she meant. It was almost the way I felt listening to Ted. But this feeling was good, clean.

"Do you feel Him, Jason? Do you?"

"Yeah. I feel Him."

I opened my eyes. Gareen smiled. Her eyes were like emeralds lit up like a Lite Brite. "Now you can pray."

"Don't know how."

"Say how you feel. Ask for help to deal with whatever comes."

I grinned at her, feeling an allover lightness. "Your father will be proud of you."

"He'll never know. Besides, I don't think we pray to the same kind of Power."

Gareen was right. I started chatting with God. It helped.

Chapter Seventeen

I needed all the help I could get. The day before court, my mind kept breaking the fear speed limit. To keep from thinking about me, I thought about Jonathan. Over and over, I replayed the court session in my mind. Jonathan sounded worse every time, like he'd been the ringleader of it all. That's not the way it was. How could we help?

Maybe Joey would have some ideas. I called him. He agreed Jonathan was going to get the worst rap. "Let's get together tonight," he said.

"Where?" It's hard for teens to find a private place in a small town. In cold, rainy weather it's almost impossible.

Joey called back a few minutes later. He'd called Gareen. I should have thought of that. Gareen would get the key to her father's church, for a "youth meeting." She didn't tell him the youths were all waiting to go to jail.

The night turned colder, wetter. Rain flooded the ditches, soaked through our coats. We filed into the church basement.

Charts on the walls said how much money they'd raised for missionaries. Sunday school drawings covered all of one wall. We got a table from a stack in a corner. Everyone grabbed a chair. The chairs and table looked like the ones in court.

"Hear ye, hear ye," Joey sang. He rang a bell he'd found on the piano. "Court is now in session." Everyone laughed.

Then we talked. Our lawyers said we'd probably get off with probation and community service. This magistrate was supposed to be tough, but we had no priors. We'd learned a lot of legal language lately. That might come in handy for Level One Canadian Law.

While we acted cheerful, I knew the real punishment would come from the long memory of our small town. Everyone would always remember we'd been "in trouble." No matter what else we did for the rest of our lives, they'd remember.

"Guys. What are we going to do about Jonathan?" I glanced around the table. He'd soon be here. I wanted to talk before he came.

"What can we do?" Tom rocked back on his chair.

"Yeah. What can we do?" Tony echoed. "He should've got a lawyer."

"We could talk to the magistrate," I said. "Before court."

"That's risky," Gareen pointed out. "It could make your own cases worse. Check with your lawyers."

Joey looked at each of us, one by one. "They'd warn us to keep our mouths shut." We nodded in agreement.

I was thinking hard. "We should try to do something. Anything. Joey, what if we went to the Hall early, by ourselves, no lawyers, no parents. Maybe the magistrate would listen then. If we explained it wasn't all Jonathan's fault. That we were all in it together."

"We could do that." Mike bowed his head into his hands. "If I'd never set up that deal, maybe this wouldn't have happened."

"Mike, Ted would have got the stuff." Vince spoke up. "He's been doing fine without you ever since. Got his own supply line set up now. He's dealing himself."

"Not guilty. Hah." Paul tapped his fingers. "I should've brought some chips. I bet Ted will get off."

"Sooner or later," Gareen said, "he'll go too far. Just wait."

Joey stretched and went over to the piano, lifted the cover off the keys, played *Chopsticks*. "Three years of piano lessons. All I remember. Oh, then there's those two." He played *Mary had a Little Lamb* and *Frère Jacques*. By this time, we'd all formed a half-circle around the piano, watching him.

Joey turned, closing the circle, pulling us together. "Will we try to help Jonathan? Talk to the magistrate in the morning? Try to tell him what really happened?"

I nodded, yes. Mike did, too.

"Sure."

"We're game." Tom and Tony were in.

Paul and Vince would go with the crowd.

The back door rattled. Jonathan roared, "Are you letting me in, or do I have to pull this door down?"

"You realize," Gareen directed her question to me, "you might hurt yourselves by doing this?"

"Yes. But we've got to do something."

The others said "Yeah" and "That's the breaks," or agreed by nodding.

Gareen smiled at us all. She ran quickly up the stairs to open the door. Jonathan and Charlotte joined us.

"Come on into the kitchen, youth group," Gareen ordered. She put the kettle on, made hot chocolate, passed around sandwiches and cookies. "Compliments of my mother. Mom and Dad are glad to see me taking an interest in pastoral care." She grinned at me. I held up my mug in a toast.

We sat around, chatted, pretended we were a normal bunch of teenagers on a normal night.

Mom had asked me to come home early. At ten I got ready to leave. The others followed my lead. We split up outside. After we walked Gareen home, Jonathan and Charlotte walked me home. Jonathan wasn't saying anything. He frowned the whole way. When we stopped by my gate, I asked them in.

"No. Not tonight." He gazed at Charlotte, she at him; I felt in the way, but I didn't want to go in yet. We stood by my picket fence and talked.

"I mightn't show up in the morning." Jonathan poked his hands into his pockets. Hunched his shoulders. "They're going to lock me up. Probably for years. My old man says it's my own fault. He's right, I guess." He stared down the street, like he wasn't seeing anything. "I'm 18. Probably go to the Pen. Can't take that."

Charlotte turned him around so she was looking straight at him. "Listen here, sonny boy. You're showing up at court. I'm not going out with a guy on the run. And where're you going to run? You're stuck on this island. Unless you're hiding a boat or a plane somewhere. No, Jonathan. There's nowhere to run. Place is too small to get lost." She shook him gently. "You're going to face the music. After it's over and done with, you can start fresh."

"If anyone lets me."

"I'll let you."

"I'm not much of it, you know, Charlotte." He looked at me flashing a sudden grin. "I fail in school. Fight when I get the chance. Hang around with bad company. Like Jason."

"I know who and what you are, Jonathan." She put her arms around his neck and looked him straight in the eyes. "I believe in you. I love you."

"This is getting too sweet and sticky for me," I said. "Good night."

Jonathan swivelled, putting his arm around Charlotte's waist, hers around his. "Good night," they said together.

I looked out the window after I went inside. They walked down the road looking like they never had a care in the world. Looking like tomorrow was never going to come.

Chapter Eighteen

Tomorrow came too soon. It took some talking to our parents (Mom wanted to go with me), but Joey, Mike, Vince, Paul, Tom, Tony and I all met at the Hall an hour before court. The magistrate stepped out of his long, black Crown Royale.

When he saw us, he pushed up his bifocals and frowned at us. He passed us on the steps. He never said a word, just unlocked the door and went inside. Before he had a chance to close the door, we all followed.

We surrounded him just inside the door, by the bulletin board with the fire regulations. He had seemed tall up at his stand, but now I saw he was short, with a pot belly. Without his gown, he looked ordinary. He had to look up at most of us.

And there were seven of us and one of him. If we turned on him, he didn't have a chance. I caught Joey's eye, had the feeling he was thinking the same thing. The rest were waiting for us to make a move. Just for a second, I imagined the magistrate's expression if we grabbed him, did something like strip him, poked him outside with nothing on. I wondered what he'd do if one of us started hitting. Or kicking. He wouldn't have a chance. Guys like him always think they're in charge. But that's because guys like us let them run the show.

Vince stared at me. Mike shuffled. Joey shook his head, no. I snapped out of it. We wouldn't have a chance afterwards, either. No. We weren't that dumb. Besides, it wouldn't be a fair fight. He was outnumbered. I'd never hurt anyone who didn't have a chance to fight back.

The magistrate was used to dealing with all kinds. He kept his cool pretty good—considering the way we crowded in on him. He took his time unbuttoning his raglan. He set his briefcase on the floor, made a bit of space around him. "What do you think you're doing?" he asked gruffly. He kept his voice level, acted like he was boss.

"Let's give him some air," Joey said. He waved his hand and we all stepped back, widened our circle. Somehow, that made the magistrate look more alone than ever. He held himself very straight, made himself look taller.

I spoke up. "Sir, we wanted to talk with you for a few minutes. Before court starts."

"Very well. This is highly irregular. Since you obviously seem to have something to say, go ahead."

I'd gone over and over what to say. Now the words got all muddled in my mind. I didn't know where to begin. "It's about Jonathan."

"Ah, yes. Jonathan. Jonathan Thomas. Your ringleader."

"Sir, that's not true." I was stuck, didn't know what to say next.

Joey tried. "He wasn't the real leader. He got caught up in it. Like us. He just happened to be at the front."

This wasn't working. No one wanted to say it was Ted who put us up to it. Our gang doesn't tattle. Not even Vince.

The magistrate kept frowning. "What is your point?"

Joey tried again. "Sir, have you ever been to a major hockey game?"

"Yes...Montreal Forum. Playoffs."

"Then you know what it's like when the Canadiens score and someone starts the screaming and the jumping up and down. It doesn't matter who the first screamer was. It happens. It's why you're there in the cold, cramped up, hardly seeing the ice, instead of nice and comfortable at home in your living room watching TV."

"I fail to see the connection."

"It might sound like Jonathan was our leader. He wasn't." Joey paused, not mentioning Ted. "He didn't get us stirred up."

"You testified this Jonathan said 'Let's go,' that he was at the forefront of your parade down Main Street, that he helped gain access. How can you say he was not your leader?"

"It wasn't that simple." None of us knew how to help Joey. "It wasn't all his fault. Or most of his fault. He was in front but we put him there."

"Young man. I advise you to stop right there. You are on the edge of causing me to re-evaluate my decision about *you*. And your friends." The magistrate was in control again. He broke through our circle between Paul and Vince. He hung up his raglan. His voice was smoother. "You have not said anything to make me see your friend in a more favorable light. Was this his idea?"

We answered with a chorus of "No's" and "he doesn't know anything about this."

The magistrate opened his briefcase. Took out his black gown. "If you have nothing more to add, I suggest that you be seated. I also suggest that you leave defence to professionals. Perhaps, if your friend had consented to having an appointed counsel, he might have fared better. Trying to defend himself has demonstrated his arrogance." He put a portfolio of papers on the table by the stand. He sat down and ignored us.

We all went outside feeling worse than ever, hoping we hadn't turned him against Jonathan even more. It's too bad real life is not more like TV where things always turn out right. There grown-ups listen to what young people have to say. We sat on the grey-painted wooden steps, not talking, waiting until our parents came to take us inside.

Chapter Nineteen

I sat between Paul and Ms. Robbins. I wished Magistrate Cook would hurry up and be done with it. He shuffled papers, cleared his throat. The room was cold, damp, and the outside sky was a whitish grey. Finally, he began. He lectured for a long, long time, calling down all vandals and teenagers in general. Principals could take lessons from that man. He made my skin crawl.

"I always feel sad when I meet new members of the criminal society. I always hope it will be a one-time acquaintance. Much to my sorrow, too often, it becomes a longtime relationship."

He went on and on, as if we were lower than pond scum, worse than the bugs you find hiding under rocks. He called us parasites.

Then he got down to brass tacks. "Since you are all first-time offenders, I may be lenient." He peered at us with an ugly look. "If you ever show up in my court again, expect no mercy. I dislike criminals I get to know. You shall be dealt with alphabetically. Jason Abbott."

I clenched my fists. Mom sat up still and hard as a statue, hardly breathing. Shivers ran up and down my back. My stomach growled.

"According to your own statements and the statements of others, you were involved in this horrendous affair from beginning to end. You participated fully. Willingly. He named all the charges, even those they dropped.

"However, upon reviewing your file, I have decided to give you a chance. It appears that before this incident you had been making an effort to improve your school standings. Mr. Grimm indicated you attempted to make amends. Mrs. Barrett has been impressed by your Festival work.

"Therefore, Jason Abbott, I sentence you to eight weeks imprisonment..."

He paused, let the words sink in, let the bottom fall out of my world. I'd miss most of the first term of school. Might never catch up.

He continued. "You are also ordered to do eighty hours of community service under the supervision of Nita Barrett. The time you have spent as her committee worker and at Food Central will count as twenty-eight hours served. You will be on probation for one year. You will report to your probation officer every two weeks for the first three months and once a month thereafter, unless he decides you need closer supervision. You will have a ten-thirty curfew. You will stay away from alcohol and drugs. You will attend school on a consistent basis. You will keep the peace. Given that this is a first-time offence and given the contents of the pre-disposition reports, I have decided on leniency."

He scared me.

"Your sentence will be suspended. Breach of probation will mean immediate confinement."

I looked at Ms. Robbins. It sounded like I wouldn't have to serve time. She whispered. "Suspended sentence. You won't be going to a detention home unless you break your probation."

My part was over. Waiting to hear what would happen with my friends was almost as bad.

Basically, except for Jonathan, we all ended up with the same terms. We had to stay in town until our probation was over. We had a full year of curfew. We'd always be watched. We had to report to a stranger. We had to be oh so careful not to make a wrong move. And this was all because I hadn't wanted Ted to see me stagger. I'd let myself be easy-led. If I had my time back—

"Jonathan Thomas."

Jonathan stood up, shifting from foot to foot.

The magistrate glared at him. "You appear to have been a prime instigator of this little spree of destruction. You seem to have some quality that inspires loyalty from your cohorts. This quality should be used wisely, Mr. Thomas. Instead, you obviously abused your friends' confidence in you, abused your own power. Not only did you lead them into this ...adventure ...but you also tried to evade arrest. Breaking in and breaking out, evading capture, are separate offenses, Mr. Thomas. If you had deigned to have counsel, you would realize this and the possible consequences of such actions.

"Do you realize, that a *man* of eighteen could be sent to

prison for more than fourteen years?"

Jonathan's face was blood-red. He looked at one of the small windows, glanced at the door guarded by a policeman.

"You are the oldest of this gang of ruffians. Therefore, you should have better sense."

We all waited. No one even coughed. My breath caught in my throat, as if a noose was drawing tight around my neck.

The magistrate went on and on. By this time, the heaters had kicked in full force. The room was boiling hot. We'd been in this room since Adam and Eve left Eden. We'd be there until the world exploded into a Black Hole. Every word aimed at Jonathan hit me.

Finally, the magistrate's wind-up key gave out. "Given that you have no prior record, that you have given of your time and labour to, one, repair the damage at Food Central, and, two, to help on a community event, given that your father replaced the broken window, I have decided to be lenient."

Someone coughed. I crossed my fingers and toes. I heard the words, "two-year sentence."

He went on. "I emphasize that your actions are not excusable. I believe a young person can be given a second chance. I do not believe it would be in your best interests to be sent to the penitentiary. At this time. Therefore, Jonathan Thomas, your two-year sentence on the first charge is suspended. On the second charge, you are to be confined for a period of four months, at the Men's Correctional Institute."

He also gave Jonathan the same restrictions and probation as the rest of us. He had to do ten more hours of service besides what he had already served. The magistrate said that, given Jonathan's age and school record, he had the option on release of either "finding gainful employment" or going back to school.

A couple of thoughts kept bouncing around in my head. It's not fair. It's not fair. He's no worse than us.

Jonathan's mother gave him an awkward, brief hug before the police led him away. His father said, "Next time, boy, you're on your own."

The rest of us kept quiet as we left the courtroom. I was glad to go home with my mom. But I felt guilty because I wasn't going with Jonathan. I was sorry we'd been such idiots.

We'd hurt ourselves, our parents, our friendship, and our reputations. Forever. Thinking about the rules we had for the next year bugged me like crazy. It was the same as being half locked up for twelve months.

Charlotte waited outside. The cops let her talk with Jonathan for a few minutes before they ordered him into the blue and white car. He stared straight ahead when they drove away.

Mom's old car had never felt so good. I wondered how Ted would be treated.

Chapter Twenty

A judge and jury declared Ted Dawson "Not Guilty." Me and the other guys were called as witnesses. The prosecutor asked me if Ted had been in the store. I said, yes. He asked if Ted had been drinking and using drugs. I said, yes. He asked if Ted had purchased any of the alcohol or drugs. I said, yes. Then he asked if Ted had been inside the store. I said, yes.

Ted's lawyer asked me right off if Ted and I got along well together. "Not really," I said.

His lawyer looked at the jury. "I see."

He asked me if I'd brought beer along. I said, yes. He asked me if we'd had beer before we met Ted. I said, not as much.

"Just answer the questions," he ordered.

Ted claimed he'd never been inside, that he'd gone along with us because he was afraid not to, but that he'd backed out before going in. I guess, since he shopped there, fingerprints wouldn't have proved much.

D. JEAN YOUNG

Ted was smooth as silk. He got the benefit of the shadow of doubt. Suzanne heard someone from the jury say Ted came across as a nice, young man who had fallen in with bad company.

It wasn't fair. We all should have got the same rap. Me, Ted, Jonathan and the rest, too.

Jonathan was always on my mind. Nights were awful. It took ages to fall asleep. When I did I'd dream I was in a locked black box. Some nights Mom woke me up to stop my screaming.

Dear Jonathan, I'd write. I'd get stuck and I'd draw rows and rows of boxes. Shaded in black and grey.

Nita Barrett put me to work right away. "You can get most of your hours done before school starts again." She said crime should be punished, even if she did like me. She found me some pretty crummy jobs. For ten days, each morning and evening, I cleaned and painted outdoor toilets at the Lakeside Camping Park. Some folks made pretty gross messes.

In a grey fog, I did my work, watched TV, went to bed. I never even called Gareen or Melissa. I thought about Melissa while I painted picnic tables in The Park.

Ted strolled by and stopped. "Having fun, Jason?" He wore brand new jeans and an expensive Far West jacket. He watched me brush Olympic Stain over all the dirty words, all the initials, all the summer memories. He took me away from my cool, cloudy mood. I was liking the late summer air, the scent of stain, the shadows of rustling leaves.

I ignored Ted. He hated that. He flicked his Bic, lit his cigarette. Kept watching me. He'd look good with a can of paint over him, I thought. Breach of probation. No. He

111

wouldn't get the satisfaction. Instead, I said. "Have a seat, Ted. Watch me have fun."

Ted took a long draw of his smoke. He blew rings straight at me. "Think I will." He sat on a bench chair, winced a bit when his back touched the bench back. Oops, I thought. He knows. He watched me finish one table, move to another.

Perfect! I painted a big piece of cardboard with the words WET PAINT. I walked over to Ted and put the sign on his bench.

He scowled and touched the bench with his left hand, stared at the brown smear.

For the first time since our sentencing, I laughed. Ted hated being teased. Tom and Tony used to drive him nuts. "This time, Ted, my boy, you're caught red-handed. Or brown-handed."

He yanked off his jacket, glared at the neat, brown stripes on the white. His backside was streaked, too. He put his jacket on, threw his cigarette at me. I laughed as he stomped away. I threw the brush into the air. Hummed as I painted.

After that, I came alive. Maybe the courts had called Ted not guilty. Everyone in town knew the difference. My dream boxes let in a bit of light around the seams. My doodles became boxes with the lids pried open. I kept worrying about Jonathan. I wouldn't rest until I saw him again.

One day, Nita sent Joey and me to clean up the beach. It was a dreary, cool day. At least no one was around. People stared at us and whispered when we did our slave labour in public.

Armed with garbage bags and sticks with stabbers on the end, we walked to the beach. We worked and chatted together. The water had washed up condoms, tampons, an animal skull, driftwood.

When the sun came out, Joey stopped. I sat down with him on a long, rotten, fallen tree. Big, black carpenter ants crawled around us. They don't bite. Joey casually showed me a couple of joints.

"Joey! That's a breach of probation. You can land in jail."

"Ah...I'll never last the full year. I'll skip classes. Stay out too late. Smoke grass. They'll haul me in. Try one."

My hand itched; I almost took the joint. "No, thanks."

"Jason, I'd just as soon be inside now. Can't stand being tied to rules. Besides, what's the difference? Walls are everywhere." He lit up, closed his eyes, inhaled with a long, deep breath.

He floated away from me, to some world of his own. I wanted to go with him. His stowed-away joint called to me.

Joey opened cloudy eyes, sized up the scene around him. He picked up a battered, Dairy Queen, peanut-buster parfait cup. Ants crawled around and over him. Slowly, carefully, he picked one ant, trapped it with the cup. The ant crept around the circle of plastic, climbed the walls, circled again, crawled down the sides. Joey melted a small hole in the bottom. He sucked on his twisted smoke, blew small puffs of the smoke into the hole. "Try it." He spoke softly. The ant slowed down. "You ever wonder what ants think, Jason? What they feel?"

"No, Joey. Never. Let's go back to work." Joey shared his smoke with the ant, forgot me and our work. I gave up on him and went to work myself.

I remembered a TV show about ants. The male who flew the highest got to mate; then he died. The queen found a dark spot, clipped her wings, and stayed there forever laying eggs. Who had the better deal, the male or the queen? She lived in the dark, never moved. Maybe the blind female workers were the winners. They went bravely out into the open world, hunting food, dragging home their dead, fighting, dying, living.

I worked alone and wondered about ants. When I went back to Joey, he blew the last puff of his second joint at his prisoner. He lifted the cup.

She circled, not noticing her freedom right away. She staggered through the golden sand on her secret quest. Just like Super Mario.

"Joey. I don't want them to lock you away."

He smiled at me. "I know, Jason. I'm sorry."

A cloud covered the sun just then; a shiver passed over me. Summer was almost over. School was going to be tough. I couldn't wait for the Festival. That would mark the end of this mixed-up summer. I'd have my hours in by then, and Jonathan would almost have his time all served. I hoped I could stay away from trouble.

Chapter Twenty-One

Before school started, Mom took me to the mall in the city to buy some clothes. If I spotted someone I knew, I'd put a few racks of clothes between me and her. Other guys did the same thing. I also talked Mom into buying me an electric razor. "It's a lifetime thing, Mom."

"I s'pose you're right. You are getting a bit ratty looking. My baby's growing up." She looked at all the different brands. "George should help you. Ah, we'll get the most expensive. Like you said, it might be a one-time deal." Mom surprised me. I'd been ready to settle for the cheapest model.

Memorial High had older girls. I'd started school with some of them. I was looking forward to high school. A lot had happened the past few months: the break-in, Melissa, Gareen, court, my first volunteer work, almost a job. Cleaning toilets. What did I want out of life? I wasn't sure yet. But I knew some things I didn't want.

When the first day of school rolled around, all things

considered, I felt good. Then I walked down the school corridors and everyone stared and whispered after I passed. I knew they were talking about me. People were meeting each other for the first time since June. I hoped it was, as my mom would say, a nine-day wonder.

I had more serious things on my mind. Last June, Ginny had said I needed certain courses for college. When I brought back *The Fuzzy Yellow Duckling*, our town librarian had given me a book about reading problems. She'd heard Ginny had been helping me. Winston Churchill and Albert Einstein had had school trouble, too. That made me feel better.

My last year's marks were low, so I was slotted for go-nowhere courses. I might not want a degree. Then again, I might. I sure didn't want to end up in a dead-end job with a boss like Ted and be afraid to leave. I might try commercial art, or something to do with math, or science. I wanted choices.

I swallowed hard, held my head high, and booked a meeting with Ginny. She'd hooked on to a one-year replacement position as Guidance Counsellor at Memorial High. I'd seen her rush through the corridors. Her new haircut and clothes looked better. Her handbag was scruffy and her shoes were clunky.

It was hard to go see Ginny. She'd probably heard of my summer adventure. She might be disgusted with me. She'd helped me before, so just maybe she cared enough to help me again.

Ginny stood up when I walked into her office. She smiled. I smiled back. Her friendship warmed me up. "Hello, Jason." She reached across her crowded desk, shook my hand. She gave my hand a little welcome squeeze before she let go. "Take some papers off that chair and talk to me."

For a minute, I didn't say anything. I was wondering what she'd heard. She seemed to guess what I was thinking.

"Yes, Jason, I know what you've been up to this summer. I can't say I'm pleased. Want to give me your side of the story?" She gazed straight at me and kept quiet.

I wanted to tell Ginny how I felt. She listened. She let me go straight through my story from beginning to end. Just like she didn't have all kinds of work piled up.

When I finished, she said, "It sounds like this has really affected you, Jason."

"We were pretty stupid. All that came after, well, it seems like too much for one little slip-up." There. I'd said it. All along that thought had been buried, making me madder and madder. I couldn't say it to any other grown-up. Not even Mom, especially not Mom.

"Yes. I see what you're saying. You're going to be held more accountable as you grow up. Life's not always fair. Jonathan's imprisonment bothers you the most. Right?"

I nodded yes and turned away for a minute. I might start crying.

She was quiet for a moment. "You know, Jason," she said, "Jonathan is responsible for his own actions. Just as you are."

"It's not the same. I'm...stronger than he is. I think first, then act; Jonathan acts first, thinks later."

"Mmm. You may be right. Still, he could have left with Elvis. He didn't have to break that window. He could have had a lawyer."

"Yes." Now I did start to sob. Hated it. Couldn't help it.

Ginny handed me a box of tissues. "But see, Ginny, Jonathan is like this big, shaggy dog who'll do whatever the people he cares about want. He led us up Main Street because that's what we wanted." I blew my nose. "If you're going to beat the dog, you should beat the master, too."

"I hear what you're saying, Jason." She waited for me to calm down. I used half her box of tissues. She took the snotty tissues and put them into her wastepaper basket. Then she patted my hand and waited. I settled down to gaspy breathing. My chest didn't feel so tight then and the rope was gone from my throat.

"Okay, Jason. Is there anything else you'd like to talk about?" She was crisp, businesslike, as if everything was normal; as if she was showing me how different sounds were written. I needed that. I took a few more tissues, blew hard into them. She poured us strong, bad-tasting coffee. I drank it. I hate coffee.

I pulled out the list of courses my teachers had given me. "Yes. There's something else. My marks up to now have been the pits. I want to try academic math, not general. And I want to try a science course, too. I might want to try university. Or something."

Ginny smiled at me. "Good. You're thinking of your future." She glanced over the sheet and chewed on her pen. "I'll see what I can do. You should be okay in math. Maybe you'd better work on your reading skills before you try the sciences. You can start those next year. You'll be a long way ahead by then. The more you do, the easier it will get. You should be able to handle this literature." She made some notes. "I'll see what I can do. I'll recommend the changes.

After that, Jason," she looked straight at me, "it's up to you. Will you give this your best shot?"

"Yes."

"Great. I'll help you as much as I can, Jason, but mostly you'll be on your own. It won't be easy. Are you ready to do more work than you've ever done?"

"I want to try."

"Good. You deserve the chance." She smiled at me again. "You can do it, Jason. Believe me. Despite your summer escapade, you've come a long, long way since last September."

I left her office feeling good. In the bathroom, I splashed cold water on my face. If anyone asked why my nose was red, I'd say I had a cold—or that I was allergic to school. I knew my record had followed me, but this was a new school and the teachers here didn't hang around with those from junior high. I'd have to get in good with them while they were still hanging on to their mellow, summertime mood.

Chapter Twenty-Two

I don't love teachers in general, but most will give a guy a chance if he keeps quiet and doesn't stir up trouble.

When the sun hit my desk, I'd want to cut class. I'd write imaginary notes: *Dear Sir, Jason had a cold yesterday so he stayed home. Marsha Evans.* It was tempting. Ginny was right. My courses were tough. My reading was still slow. I needed to listen, to depend on my memory.

When we had a homeroom election for Student Council, Tom nominated me, like he did every year. We sort of considered ourselves the local Rhino Party. Gareen and Adam Dunbar ran, too.

It was dumb to hold an election in the first week of school. New students from all three nearby towns were bussed into Memorial High. We were just getting to know each other. Each of us had to give a speech, then the class voted. No one campaigned.

Gareen spoke first. She said she wanted to make sure

students were heard when important decisions were made.

Neat Adam, in his buttoned-up, striped blue and white shirt, said, "I'm a good debater." That was true. "I'll be the best *man* for the job." He rubbed his chin when he said MAN. He went on with a few other I-I-I and me-me-me statements.

It was my turn. I'd planned to make people take me seriously this year. My tongue got away from me. I said, "I promise to try to legalize gum chewing. I'll work for longer recess times, longer lunch hours, more holidays, shorter classes and no exams."

Everyone laughed and cheered. Our homeroom teacher taught us English, too. Mr. Silversteen had dark, oily hair. He wore a striped T-shirt, jeans and, best of all, a black eyepatch. We called him Long John Silver. His one eye sized me up. He looked out at the September sunshine, sighed, "I wish you luck."

Out of the twenty-four students in our class, eleven people, including me, voted for Gareen. Seven people voted for me! That was crazy! Adam Dunbar got six votes. We all clapped for Gareen.

Long John said, "We need a second ballot. Gareen doesn't have a clear majority. Adam's name will be dropped from the ballot and you'll all vote again."

Gareen grinned at me. "Let's go for it."

I was tempted. "I've got a better idea," I said. Me and Pop had watched leadership conventions on TV. I knew how it should be done. "Let's make Gareen's election unanimous. I can be her deputy. She has to consult me on important issues. Like parties. Longer recess times. Shorter classes."

"Agreed," she said.

Everyone cheered.

After class, Gareen caught up with me. As usual I was one of the first out the door. "Thanks, Jason. You might have won, you know. It's a new ballgame this year. All the old cliques are split. Anything can happen." She smiled up at me.

Melissa joined us. For a few seconds the same old glow that we'd shared came back. Our magic triangle. Joey's words at the beach jingled in my mind. "Triangles, everywhere. Pyramid power. Pyramids can do anything."

The twerp, Adam Dunbar, crashed in on our little meeting. "Congratulations, Gareen." He ignored me. "Melissa, come to the biology lab with me. I've got to show you something."

She hesitated. "Come on. It's really something." She shrugged and went with him. She could have stayed and talked a minute. But she went with Adam. He was growing sea monkeys. I'd heard him tell Ted at the lockers.

We watched them walk away. Gareen asked, "You okay?"

"Sure. It was just a summer romance, nothing serious."

"Sure. Tell that to another sucker." Gareen looked at her schedule. "Gym next. I'd better hurry. Thanks again, Jason."

My next class was...I checked my schedule...algebra. Good. I'd never tell anyone, but I liked figuring out how x and y fit together. It was like a puzzle. I liked computer class, too—especially the spell check on Word Perfect.

At Memorial High, we changed classes and classmates five times a day. I liked that better than staying in one place all day with the same kids and the same teacher. It would be easier to cut class, too. I tried not to think of that.

Thinking of the outside made me think of Jonathan. He'd been inside three weeks now. He must be going nuts. I still couldn't write. Mike and I wanted to visit Jonathan, but Mike's old car boiled over if he went more than ten miles. He might get a "good deal" for a used radiator. Maybe we'd get there next weekend.

Charlotte drove out once a week, but Jonathan was only allowed one visit a day. She taught him exercises he could do in a small space. Jonathan in a small space! I didn't want to think about that.

Elvis had quit and found a factory job on the mainland. The rest of our gang found their own ways to deal with high school. Tom and Tony traded places; they each went half-time. Vince and Joey hardly ever came. Ginny was helping Mike. Paul was having a good time eating mistakes people made in cooking class. We never saw each other much because our schedules were all different.

Ted's locker was next to mine but I didn't want to talk with him. He'd speak to me but I'd keep imagining ways to make him pay for his part in our break-in. It didn't seem fair for him to get off so easy.

There were times when he'd be talking to a crowd and they'd be listening to the way only Ted could tell a story. I'd want to go over and listen, too. He could make any time feel like a lazy summer day when he put his voice down low and got you listening hard. I missed the listening.

After awhile, Ted ignored me. He found a new group. Paul and Vince hung out with him. Ted was into selling dope. I wanted far away from that.

Then one day I realized Ted had paid a price for the break-in after all.

123

We had to change for gym. Ted was always the last to go on the floor. This time I went back to the washroom after the other guys had gone out. I just knew if I didn't pee I'd never make it around the gym for all those laps Coach loved to give us.

Ted's T-shirt had fallen off the stall where he changed. He opened it and bent to pick it up before he realized I was there.

Coach poked his head in from the gym door. "Come on. Move it!" He yelled. "Both of you. Twenty laps each and fifty push-ups for both of you. Another two minutes and I'll double that!"

When Ted turned to look at the coach, I saw his bare back. I'd never seen him without his shirt before. Not even at the beach. He'd never gone swimming. Scars covered Ted's back. Some scars were barely healed over. Neat rows of deep welts. Mom's words about the cat-o'-nine tails came back to me.

Ted saw my face when he looked back at me. It hit him all

of a sudden what his back looked like. "You see, Jason, I paid." Ted looked pitiful, standing almost naked in the blaring light.

"Ted, no one has to put up with that stuff. That's abuse."

"Oh? So what do I do, Jason? Report him? Then what? He'd lose his career. They'd ship me off to a foster home."

I didn't know what to say.

He went on. "Report him, Jason? Where would I be then? Fatherless. Poor. Like you."

He knew how to hurt. I wasn't poor any more, but I had no father. My mom was a lot better than a father like that.

Ted kept talking. He must have wanted to get it all out of the way; it was strange. He picked up for his father. "He only hits where it won't show." He walked to the sink and turned on the cold water. He splashed some on his eyes and shivered. The welts on his back turned a dark purple. "Abbott, if you ever tell anyone about this, you're dead meat."

The coach poked his head in. "That's it! Double laps."

"Sir," I said, "Ted's not feeling well. I thought he was going to faint."

The coach glared at Ted. Ted leaned back against the sink, his face still wet. "Get lost, Ted, go lie down somewhere. You look peaked. Be on time next class. Or else." He pointed at me. "As for you, Abbott, get out there!"

I went as soon as I used the urinal. Ted stayed holding on to the sink like he was afraid it might give way from under him.

While I ran my forty laps, I thought of the way Ted's father had rubbed his belt the night they picked him up. I remembered how Ted had looked when they left the jail.

Later that day, Charlotte called. "Great news! Jonathan's coming home this weekend. I'm picking him up. Time off for good behaviour."

A weight lifted off me. My box split wide open. The Autumn Leaves Festival was week after next. Then summer was really over. We had a lot to do. I'd get my hours done, no sweat.

Chapter Twenty-Four

"Nita, I'll work hard finishing up the Festival project. That'll wipe out my hours. Right?"

"Maybe I shouldn't allow this." She frowned at me. "It's something you want to do and that's not punishment. I've heard about Melissa and Gareen."

I was sick of crummy jobs. "I need to get the hours over with. School's getting really tough."

She made us hot tea and took a pan of blueberry muffins from her oven. "Okay," she said. "Here's your last two hours. One, target for the cream pie toss. Two, the dunk tank."

"Nita! I'll miss the best of the Festival. I'll freeze."

"Don't worry. If it's too cold, I'll find you something worse to finish off your sentence."

"Thanks a lot."

"Your last two hours are set in stone. Anything extra is volunteer work. The recording angel will write it in her good book."

I pretended to think it over. "Okay, but if it's too cold for the tank, I want to finish up at the Festival anyway." She passed me the butter. I split open my muffin, watched the Eversweet melt.

"I suppose that's only fair but, Jason, I want you to remember your service. I don't want to hear you're into trouble again. Ever."

"I'll be a good boy, Nita." I folded my hands and bowed my head. "I'll be an angel."

She laughed. "That'll be the day." She reached across the table, patted my arm. "Jason, I'll have your curfew moved to twelve-thirty for that night. That way you can go to the dance."

"Thanks, Nita. Could you do that for my friends, too?"

"I'll see what I can do."

"Jonathan's coming home this weekend."

"He can work at the Festival but I won't put *him* on the dunk tank. He's had it worse than you."

Contrary-like, I said, "That's not fair."

"Go home, Jason. Don't push your luck." She stood up. I was dismissed.

I took an extra muffin on the way out and left Nita's, whistling. Getting slammed in the face with cream pie or taking cold water dips would be gross. But, hey, then my hours would be done. I'd just have another ten months of curfew and check-ins with my probation officer and staying in town.

I couldn't wait to see Jonathan. Things were looking good. I never expected the snags that came.

Chapter Twenty-Five

Sunshine and a perfect, September-blue sky woke me up on Saturday morning. No one else stirred in my house or on the streets. Maples flashed neon red, fluorescent orange. Birch leaves glowed pale green, bright yellow. Summer flashed its closing out sale.

When I reached Gareen's house, she opened the door before I pressed the button. Her old, green sweater hung down to her knees over paint-stained jeans. She joined me, smiling, carrying a battered, brown vinyl bag full of tools. She gave me another bulging bag. Her red hair caught the sun; it was perfect for this day. Its waves fell in a sloppy, careless, no-style. We didn't need to talk.

We walked to the field outside the stadium. We'd set up the booths inside. If the weather was fine next weekend, we'd set up outside early Saturday morning. If it was cold or rainy, the Festival would be held inside.

The stadium smelled dusty. They closed it up after the

summer sports program. In November, they'd flood the floor, make ice. Our footsteps echoed on the cement. Dust floated in the air. The place had a big, empty, church kind of feeling.

We checked all the boards we'd painted for damage and started in right away. We drew chalk designs on the floor and argued a lot. Around ten o'clock, we sat in the penalty box and drank Pepsi. We were still the only ones there.

I grumbled. "Melissa's parents shouldn't get in our way."

Gareen sipped her warm Pepsi. "Don't kid yourself."

"What do you mean?"

"She'd see you if she really wanted to."

"How can you say that?"

"Listen. How do you think I got the freedom I've got? By agreeing all the time with Mom and Dad?"

"I don't know."

"I had to fight to go to movies, to go to a dance, for heavens sake. Even to wear make-up and I hardly use it. Jason, do you think The Preacher likes me hanging around with you?"

That stopped me cold. I'd never thought I might be a problem for Gareen. We were just friends. "What do you do?"

"Stand up for what I want. It's easier now." She ripped open a bag of salt and vinegar chips, offered me some. I took a few. "I made up my mind about four years ago I didn't want to live like my parents. I believe in God. I pray. But I don't believe in all their 'do nots.' I don't know who's going to heaven. Or hell. I went on strike."

"You went on strike? You were only—"

"Twelve. I stopped doing my homework. Went to school. Didn't pick up a pencil. Stopped making my bed, tidying my room. Put on a nice dress every day, pantihose, bra. I hated bras. Sat at the table, prim and proper, like a little doll, like a perfect lady. I did nothing."

"Wow. That must have almost killed you."

"You got that right. Dad was pleased. Mom almost died. I like doing well in school. Hate dressing up. If Dad wanted a little robot who only acted when he told me to, that's what he'd get. Finally, after a month—"

"A month!"

"He saw something was wrong. Mom got through to him. The teachers called, too."

"What happened?"

"He 'could stand it no longer.' He decided to 'leave me in the Lord's hands.' We made a deal." She munched her chips.

"Go on."

"I promised to go to church every Sunday, but not Sunday school. I promised I wouldn't cheat, steal, lie, murder—you know, the usual cardinal sins. I said I'd try not to covet. Try to honour my parents. I wanted some freedom and the right to make some choices."

"Sounds heavy for a twelve-year-old kid."

She flashed a grin at me. "Preachers' kids learn to speak up. Comes from hearing sermon after sermon and seeing sad people come for help. Dad does do a lot of good."

"Do you do what you want now? I'm impressed."

"Not quite. When I go to a dance," she offered me more chips, grinned at me, "when I 'hang around with gangsters,' we go through a rough scene. You should see what happens if I dare bring a guy home. I only did that once. The guy moved the next week. I wonder why."

"You're kidding, right?"

Gareen laughed cheerfully. "That's what you think. By the time I get clear, I'm too exhausted to be bad."

"You're strong. Melissa can't be like you."

"Melissa, again. Always Melissa. Melissa likes being weak. It's nice having someone else make decisions for you. Easy." She spoke each word, one at a time.

I paid attention and took more of her chips. I wanted to share something of me with her. I should have shut up about Melissa. I couldn't help myself. "I think of Melissa and I imagine summer roses in moonlight. I get a shivery, wanting feeling."

"You've got it bad, Jason. Give me some of your Pepsi." I passed her my can. "What do you think those moonlit summer roses will be like on a cold, November morning?"

Her words made me see a bare rosebush, standing stark, prickly, no leaves, no flowers, lonely in pale, yellow sunlight. Drifts of snow swirled around the bush. I shivered. Gareen looked at me like she knew what I was thinking.

Gareen was close, warm, and all of a sudden I wanted to know what her lips tasted like. I bent across to her, kissed her a quick, gentle kiss flavoured by Pepsi, salt and vinegar. She put her hands around my neck, kissed me back. Long and slow. We pulled back, both at the same time. I saw my surprise shining back from her eyes.

I'm in the school choir. Easy credit. Ms. Morningglory starts every class with the first three bars of Beethoven's Fifth. I've never heard the rest of it. I'd like to hear the whole thing sometime.

Gareen's kiss made me feel like that—like we were on the brink of something big and powerful; like there'd be ripples rolling around us forever if we kissed again. It scared me.

Gareen jumped up, pushed open the penalty box door. "Come on, Jason. Let's cut this foolishness and get to work."

"Hey, wait a minute, Gareen!"

"Oh, so you want me, now, Jason? Two minutes ago, you told me how crazy you were for Melissa."

I followed her. She hurled her Pepsi can into the blue box for cans. She scrunched up her chip bag, tossed it into another box. She walked so fast I could hardly keep up with her. And my long legs covered twice as much ground as hers.

"Give me a break, Gareen. Romeo was in love with someone else just before he fell for Juliet." I'd seen the videos.

She stopped. Whirled around and said, "Yes. Right. And look what happened to them!"

She had a point. Just then the door creaked open. In came Jonathan and Charlotte. I gave Gareen an "I have to talk with you later" look and ran to greet my friend.

"Hey there," he boomed. "Good to see you!" He threw his arm over my shoulders. He was a bit taller than me now. He must have grown in there.

It's too bad I can't sing, because I wanted to sing at the top of my lungs just then. Jonathan was home. He was okay. He was free.

Gareen turned real efficient. She put us all to work. Others came in, in groups of two or three. Melissa showed up around noon. She looked awfully young. When she looked at me with her long-lashed, grey eyes, I wanted to touch her, to hold her. It's a wonder her mother let her come.

For the rest of that day, I followed Gareen's orders, hardly arguing at all. The two girls were different in every way. I wanted both of them. I walked home alone. Melissa's mother picked her up. Nita Barrett praised my work. "This is going to be a great-looking Festival! Time to go home Jason. You can hoof it." She gave Gareen a ride.

That night I asked Mom, "Do you think a guy can be in love with two girls at the same time?"

"Oh my goodness. Jason. I thought you said there wasn't a single girl you liked much just a little while ago? And now you love two?" She shook her head. "What am I going to do with you?"

"Don't worry. Neither of them wants me."

"This gets better and better." She frowned. "We should talk about the birds and the bees."

"Mom! I know all about that!"

"I did, too. That's the problem. Poking and buzzing can still make little baby chicks and flowers." She took me by the shoulders. "Remember, I was your age when you were born. Too young to be a mother. Too young now to be a grandmother. You, my son, are too young to be a father."

"Gee whiz, Mom. We only kissed."

"That's how it starts. That's what the bee says when she rubs along some poor little innocent flower. I only want to touch you. It won't hurt a bit. You might even like it." She let me go, sat down at the telephone table and started dialling. All the while she muttered about birds and bees and flowers and eggs.

"Mom, you're calling your hairdresser, aren't you?"

"Yes. Then I'm making an appointment with your doctor. I'm getting him to talk to you straight about birth control. In case you don't have enough sense to keep your pants on."

The hairdresser answered. Mom made an appointment for the next day. She dialled again, talked while the rings were going in. "I want you to stop and think. No son of mine is leaving some poor girl alone with a fatherless child. If you're in love with two, then things could get real hairy."

She had a point. I went to see the doctor. He cleared up a few things for me I hadn't been sure about. He said the only 100% type of birth control was Mom's favorite—keeping your pants on. He told me about sexually transmitted diseases like herpes, syphilis, gonorrhoea. They're more common than AIDS. They mightn't kill you, but they can make life miserable. Some STDs like herpes can't ever be cured. Condoms aren't 100% safe but they're a whole lot better than nothing. Latex are best.

It was all pretty gross. He had a plastic model of a man's parts and he showed me "the proper way" to use these things. He gave me a pack of samples. Just in case.

I guessed it was better to be informed. He'd made it easy by acting like sex was no big deal. For now the 100% solution made sense. But like Mom said, you never know. I knew a couple of things for sure—I didn't want to be called Daddy for a long time yet. I wanted to be there for my kids. I know how it feels when you don't know your real father.

CHAPTER TWENTY-SIX

Jonathan called me on Sunday morning. We went to the rocky part of the beach, just the two of us. We kicked off our deck shoes, pulled off our socks, rolled up our jeans, and sat on a low, flat rock we called The Chair. The Chair is a flat rock jutting out from two bigger boulders. We dangled our feet in the cold water. Fat, fluffy clouds decorated the blue sky. Cumulus. I learned that in Environmental Science.

We watched sea gulls playing, gliding on the light breeze. "What was it like, Jonathan, inside?"

Jonathan swished his hand in the water. "Boring. Paul might have liked it, if there was more to eat. Nothing to do. All day. Every day. Meals, same time, same taste. Same faces. Pacing back and forth in this tiny, little cell. Or hallways. Television. I hate television. Same thing, over and over."

He splashed water on his face. Took a deep breath. I thought of Ted for just a second. Jonathan went on. "Almost went nuts. Would've gone nuts, if it wasn't for Charlotte. She wrote me every day. They read your letters, you know, so there's not everything you can say. Charlotte visited me every Saturday. Look, she showed me isometric exercises." He demonstrated, flexing muscles I didn't know we had. "Two hours a day, they let us out into this 'exercise yard.' About 400 square metres of yellow grass."

"Do you think it did you any good at all, Jonathan? Did you learn anything?"

"Hah. One guy told me how to hotwire a car. I'll never be stuck for a ride. Found out who deals where. Another fellow told me how to shoplift. Go in pairs. One guy kicks up a fuss or breaks something 'accidentally' to sidetrack the clerks. The other makes off with the loot. I know who to contact for dope. Yeah. I learned a few things. They won't do me much good."

He reached way down into the water, picked up a small, round rock. Tossed it casually into the waves. "Maybe Joey can get off on staring at stains, or bars. Not me."

"When are you going back to school, Jon? If you don't start soon, you'll never catch up."

He laughed loud and hearty. I'd missed that laugh. "Jason, I haven't caught up in years. Promoted without a diploma. Big deal."

"Listen. I bet Ginny could help you. Last year I couldn't hardly read."

"She could help you. You're smart. You want to learn that school junk. I could see you caught on to stuff, even if you couldn't put it on paper. I can read but I don't want to."

We were quiet, then. A sea gull grabbed a prize from another. Jonathan said, "I'm never starting school again."

I didn't know what to say.

"There's a storm coming up out on the ocean. That's why the gulls are in. That's what my old man always says." Jonathan pushed his feet right down to the rocks.

I did the same and made my jeans wet. The rocks under my feet were smooth, worn down by the water.

Jonathan kept talking. A lot must have been bottled up. Most times, he's more of a doer than a talker. "I'm released into the custody of Charlotte's father. My old man probably figures I should've served the full term. They never called me once. Never wrote. Never came to see me. Charlotte told me about Mike's car."

"I tried to write. Couldn't get the words down."

"That's okay. I never even wrote Charlotte and I had loads of time. I'm living with Charlotte and her dad."

"Jon, come back to school. I'll help. Give it a try."

"Nope. Never wanted to be there in the first place. Can't stand schoolwork. I'm not going back."

"What are you going to do then?"

"Help Charlotte's dad set up his fitness centre. He'll pay me minimum wage to start and a share in the profits when the place gets rolling."

"What if it doesn't work out? What if you and Charlotte split? Or you get to hate her old man?"

"That won't happen."

"But if it does?"

"I'll worry about that if the time ever comes." Jonathan leapt up onto the top of the highest rock. His voice carried across the waves, echoed. "I'm finished with school. Finished! Remember, Jason, remember when we were little? 'I'm the king of the castle, you're the dirty rascal!'"

I looked up at him. He stood over me, tall, big, highlighted against the blue sky. Looking strong, powerful. I wasn't a bit worried about Jonathan.

I jumped off the flat rock, ran along the beach. The smooth rocks hurt my bare feet. I picked up a flat, black rock and skipped it across the waves. The rock jumped three times.

Jonathan laughed. He hopped down and ran past me. He picked out his own small, flat rock. He threw back his arm and his isometrically-tuned muscles popped. He flung that rock with forty-two days of caged-up energy. I stopped counting the bounces at nine. The rock danced far out over the waves. I never saw it sink. Maybe it kept leaping forever.

Jonathan slapped me on the back and laughed. "Beat that with your math and your physics, Jason."

CHAPTER TWENTY-SEVEN

On the morning of the Festival, Gareen walked to the stadium with me. The sun was warm on our backs. I wondered if we'd sit in the penalty box together. Without talking about it, we'd gone past that and stayed friends. Romance might ruin everything. I wondered if Melissa would be there. Since we'd kissed, I didn't feel like talking about Melissa to Gareen.

Sherri had looked up from her early morning cartoons when I left. "You should shave, Jason. You look like Super Mario." I went back to check in the bathroom mirror. My moustache was filling in. After waiting for it for years, I wasn't about to shave it off yet.

A crowd showed up just after we got there. By twelve everything was set up. I wished I could take it easy, bum around in the afternoon. Talk to everyone, enjoy the Festival.

Nita said, "Get the pies and the dunk tank over with."

I'd been thinking about the dance all week. Even though

there'd be beer and hard liquor, we all had special permission to go, thanks to Nita. A night to stay out late. That would sure feel good.

Melissa was going with Adam Dunbar. He'd volunteered just enough to get in free.

When we broke for lunch, I got up my nerve. "Gareen, will you go to the dance with me?"

She looked up from her ham sandwich. "Sure. We'll hang out together."

"Gareen, I want to take you, like on a date."

She froze. Blushed. Took another bite. Chewed it slowly. I held my breath, afraid to push her.

"Okay. We can try it. As long as we can still be friends. Even if it doesn't work out."

I held out my hand. "We'll shake on it."

At one o'clock I stuck my head through the hole. Little children lined up to fling creamy pies at the "funny tree face." I had drawn a big tree in the middle of smaller ones with faces looking up at the centre hole. We'd covered it with clear plastic so the paint wouldn't get mussed up by the cream. I'd never expected to be the target. I should have made the hole higher. My neck got stiff real fast. Half of the time, the kids missed. They laughed so hard at their direct hits, I didn't mind their smacks.

Melissa collected the money for the Heart and Stroke Foundation. She wiped my face between pies. She giggled a lot, cheered when a kid scored. Her soft hands gently cleaned off the cream. It was pure, sweet torture.

After half an hour, my neck sure hurt. Line-ups stayed long. At twenty minutes before two, Ted came by. He stopped when he realized I was the target. "Well. Look at the funny face!"

He handed Melissa a ten-dollar bill. "I'll take ten plates, Melissa. Jason looks hungry."

"This game's for kids, Ted."

"I'm a kid at heart, 'Liss." He picked up a bunch of plates and the can of Whipped Cream."

Melissa looked at me helplessly. I moved, trying to get more comfortable. "Take his money."

She looked at the ten, sighed, and put it into her pouch. "Stand way back, Ted. Way back."

"Sure. Try to pretend I'm not alive now, Jason. Thanks to my father I'm not into this stuff like you. You don't have to take this, you know. It's abuse." Ted didn't miss once. He smashed the ten pies at me, one after another. My nose hurt by number three. I kept smiling. People gathered around and stared.

"Mmm. Delicious. More, Ted, more." He wasn't going to see me squirm. It was almost worth the misery. He walked away, shoulders held stiff, madder than ever. I'd managed to keep smiling. Melissa took a warm cloth, wiped my face. When I stood and stretched, she rubbed my neck. We were behind the tree. She kissed me quickly, gently.

"Oops!" Joey peeped at us. Melissa jumped away, blushing. Joey was here to take my place. I cleaned up, bought a moose burger and Coke from Paul. They'd made a big mistake putting him with food. The Boy Scout Jamboree lost money. Whenever Paul's coworker looked away, he ate. "This is great," Paul told me.

I was keyed up tight; I needed to freak out for a bit, to get rid of some of my energy. At Jonathan's stand (raising money for the Red Cross), I hurled a few balls at dumb, grinning, stuffed cats. They looked like Ted. I won a medium prize. Sherri might like the feathered key chain.

Nita Barrett spotted me and frowned. "It's almost two-thirty, Jason. Man your post."

It was just as well to get my last hour done. I had my bathing trunks on under my jeans. Would it be best to strip off? It was hot, especially for this time of year. I kept my shirt on. I climbed up onto the tippy perch.

For the first ten minutes, only a couple of old men gave it a shot. They missed. This wasn't so bad after all. I could see the whole field from here. Mike bagged garbage. Vince spun the wheel of fortune while a Kinsman collected money.

A couple of guys I'd started kindergarten with showed up. They were in Level Three now. We hadn't talked in years. "How's the weather up there?" asked Steve. He's short, square and silly.

"Just wonderful. Great view. Want to trade places?"

"No, thanks. You look hot. Give me a ball."

He gave Doreen Mercer, a volunteer for Laubach for Juniors, a couple dollars. He couldn't hit the broad side of a barn. Clinton, his buddy, could. He gave me my first dunking. The sun had warmed the water, but I shivered when I climbed out of the tank. The air was cooling down. My shirt stuck to my skin.

Crowds are like sharks. When they smell blood, they gather to take bites. After I hit the water once, people lined up to dunk me. Most missed. By ten past three, I'd been soaked three times. I took my shirt off—it made me colder when it clung to my body. I wished I could dunk Nita Barrett.

I climbed on the stool for the fourth time and looked down. Ted was fanning out seven two-dollar bills. He smiled his special, sleazy grin. He was getting me back for ignoring him, for knowing his secret. He was drawn to me, just like I kept wanting to be around him. That was something I couldn't explain. I bet he couldn't either.

It wasn't easy, but I smiled right back at him. "Hello, Ted. Lovely day for a swim. You should try it."

"I'm just here to watch you having fun." He missed with his first two balls.

"Poor Ted. He can't play a grown-up's game."

His smile was gone. He missed again. There were ten minutes left. I didn't like the look on his face. He held the ball up, aimed it at my head. That ball could hurt. If it hit where he aimed, he'd blacken my eye.

My hand wanted to go up to ward off the ball. If I did that, I'd lose balance and fall in anyway. I'd look like a fool.

When Ted saw I wasn't about to react, he aimed at the target. He hit a corner. The target shook, but I didn't fall.

"Poor Ted." Two could play this game.

He scored the next time. I climbed out of the tank. "Thanks, Ted. I was getting hot." I took my time drying off and climbing back up. Ted waited.

"Five minutes left." Doreen checked her watch. "Then it's Joey Ryerson's turn."

Ted had three balls left. More people came around. Someone said, "Give me a chance. You've dunked him once."

Ted hit the target right on again. A cloud covered the sun and it was cooling fast in the end-of-summer air. I shivered and sneezed when I climbed up.

Ted wasn't going to know how much I wanted to grab him, throw him in the tank. He had two balls. He aimed, saw me tense up, stopped. I forced myself to go loose. I even whistled.

A crowd was all around the tank now. Everyone was quiet, knowing something more than a bit of fun was going on. Whispers about the cream pie throw drifted on the air.

An old lady, carrying an umbrella, peered up at me. "You poor boy. You'll catch cold, sitting up there, soaking wet. I'm going to speak to someone about this!"

The cloud moved past the sun. The air felt warm again. "Thank you, ma'am. You do that." I pretended to lift a top hat, made a careful bow. People laughed and the tension snapped. Ted took aim, threw. He hit the edge of the target so my perch shook. I hung tight. The catch squeaked. I thought it might hang on, but it quivered too much and the cold wetness swallowed me.

Ted had one ball left. "Are you clean enough yet, Jason?"

He wasn't going to scare me. I climbed back up, shivering like I'd never be warm again. "It might take another rinse, Ted."

"Jason, you have two minutes left." Doreen glared at Ted.

Ted waited a full minute and a half. I know. I counted off each shivering second silently. One thousand one. One thousand two... Doreen kept an eye on her watch, Ted on his.

Everyone waited. I hummed. Tried not to let my teeth chatter. Ted waited, soaked up the crowd's attention. He aimed, fired. Bang!

The catch let go and I slid one last time into the tank. A

cold breeze made me shiver all over. This time I couldn't make my teeth stop chattering. Ted watched me, waited to see what I'd do.

I managed to smile as if what he'd done didn't matter. I bowed to my audience and everyone cheered. I dried off, put on my warm sweatshirt. The softness of the new fleece against my cold body made me feel better.

Ted swaggered off, hands clenched.

I felt like a winner. I hadn't lost my cool. At least not so anyone could tell. No one knew how hard it had been to stay loose and smiling. For years, I'd pretended not to care people thought I was stun. Maybe those years hadn't been wasted after all.

Joey was supposed to go on the tank next. "Joey, don't go up there. You'll freeze. I'll clear it with Nita."

Joey grinned at me. "Don't bother. I want to give it a try. See what it feels like." He took off his jeans, left his T-shirt on. I left him my towels and my dry T-shirt.

Before he settled onto the small seat, he said, "I got here early. They ran out of Whipped Cream. You played it cool, Jase. Real cool." He held up his fingers in a victory sign.

I left Joey to feel the joys of getting wet on a cool day. I figured my bad times were over. I never expected Ted to pull another trick. I was more worried about meeting Gareen's parents.

Chapter Twenty-Eight

At seven o'clock on the button, I rang Gareen's doorbell. She asked me in and she introduced me to her parents. Reverend Divine took my hand, squeezed it in his clergyman's grip. Her mother held my hand, gently, for a bare second.

Reverend Divine said, "Gareen must be home by twelve-thirty. Please join us for a brief prayer."

"Yes, sir."

He made us all kneel. "May the good Lord forgive these children as they head out to a place of evil. Satan's sounds and the befouling scent of cigarettes will surround them. May God guide them through this den of iniquity. Keep them from straying onto the highway to the flames of hell. Keep them on the straight, narrow road to goodness. For His own Name's sake. Amen."

Gareen twinkled a glance my way, stared at the ceiling, closed her eyes for a second. She probably prayed her own prayer. I would have.

As we left, her mother gave her two folded tens. "Call me if you need me."

The front door closed behind us. Gareen said, "Now you know. How many guys will dare face that?"

"Awesome! Simply awesome."

Gareen was a pro at handling sit-down dinners and head tables. She'd been doing this kind of thing all her life. Gareen said grace. I watched her to see which fork to use first. I felt like everyone was staring at me.

There were speeches. Nita praised us up like we were heroes. "There are many to thank tonight." She listed a lot of people. Then she said, "Three young people, Gareen Parsons, Jason Abbott and Melissa Coldburn, have worked hard with volunteers too numerous to name. They designed the booths and backdrops for this good-looking, most organized Autumn Leaves Festival."

Everyone clapped. We had to stand up. She said a bit more, talked about things I never knew she'd noticed. Nita Barrett nosed into everything.

No one had ever praised me up in public before. They only talked about the trouble I caused.

We laughed all through the Villagers' play. The sets looked perfect. Melissa and Adam sat a couple rows ahead of us. She looked back at us during intermission. We connected like we always did. "Looks good, hey? We did okay."

"Yeah. We sure did." Gareen moved slightly beside me. She never said a word.

Just about everyone in town went to the dance. The music wasn't what we'd play at young people's dances. There was a mixture for every taste. The old waltzes did give me a chance to hold Gareen close. Her body curved in against mine, soft, firm, strong. Melissa used to blend right into me. Gareen could stand on her own if I stepped back. We fit together like two halves, but I knew where I started and she began.

Gareen's hair had a scent like summer grass, clean, fresh, outdoorsy. She'd taken time to make it look pretty tonight. She had on new glasses, too. The music stopped. She stepped back from me, looked up at me. I felt a question coming. The deejay flipped through his tapes.

"Let's sit down." I took her by the hand and we sat at our table by our half-gone Coca Colas.

"Jason, how do you picture me?" She was remembering Melissa, moonlight, roses.

I thought about Gareen. "You're a red pine."

"I'm a tree? A plain old tree?"

I had a pen in my jacket pocket. I spread out my napkin and started drawing while I talked. "Not just any old tree. Red pines are endangered. They're special. No one's allowed to cut them." I sketched a tall, elegant, long-needled tree.

"I'm not tall."

"You are in spirit. Now pay attention. Unless you don't want to hear."

"Go ahead. I'm all ears."

"Hah. More tongue, I'd say."

She stuck her pink tongue out at me.

"Well, trees don't have tongues, but this one says a lot anyway. Can I go on?"

"Why not?"

"Mom said they used red pine needles to stuff pillows. They

smell good." I touched her hair, smiled. I added a nest with wide-mouthed babies, a mother bird flying to the tree with a worm. "You'd be the kind of tree birds use for summertime nests." I added clouds, notes of music. "A tree that whispers in a quiet breeze, howls in stormy winds." I added popcorn garlands, birdseed balls. Tiny birds pecked around the base of the trunk. "Little children decorate you at Christmas time." I was really into the image now. Drawing does that to me. I drew the outline of a half-hidden tree house, nailed steps onto the trunk. "You have a tree house for fun. And..." I sketched one end of a hammock trailing off the end of the napkin. I'd run out of room, "...and a hammock for rest."

The music played another slow waltz. I looked out on the dance floor. Melissa was trying to melt against Adam Dunbar. Hard to do with him. He held himself too straight. Gareen saw where I was looking. She sighed.

I looked back at my drawing, across at Gareen and finished my picture and my story of how I saw her. "On a cold November morn," I added a sun in an upper corner, tiny snowflakes dancing all around, "a red pine is as green and strong as it is in June sunshine or cool, September nights."

Gareen smiled. She folded the napkin. She didn't have a purse. She folded it real small and unbuttoned one button of her dress. Her firm breasts showed just a bit. She stuffed the napkin into her bra, watched me as she did it. Casually, she buttoned up again.

"I want to add something," I reached for her button.

"Get out of that!" She slapped my hand. A song we liked came on, a fast song. "Come on, Jason, let's dance." We danced until some old people requested a jig.

Just as the jig music started, a blast of cold air blew in from the outside. Ted, Vince, and Paul strolled into the hall. Ted scanned the room, seeing where everyone was. When he saw me, he stopped looking. I turned my back on him.

CHAPTER TWENTY-NINE

The older people were really getting into the jig. I walked Gareen back to our table. "I'll get us a Coke." I was on my way to the bar when Ted stood in my way. I stepped to one side. He stepped to one side.

"Aw, Ted, leave him alone." Paul didn't want a fight.

"Yeah. Ted, you showed him up good enough today." Vince tugged on Ted's arm. Ted shoved them both away. The door opened again. Five of Ted's new buddies came in. They all wore studded, leather jackets. They marched over, stood, two on one side of Ted, three on the other.

Our gang had gone through a time when we'd fought a lot. Won most of the fights, too. After that, no one bothered us.

I wasn't scared of Ted and his friends, but he'd always rubbed me the wrong way. Now, every nerve in my body cried, "Let me at him!"

I felt someone at my right side. Jonathan. Tom and Tony

moved in on my left. Joey came out of the bathroom. He saw the action and joined us.

Six of them. Five of us. Paul and Vince didn't count. Mike was at the bar, looking scared. We could take them. Jonathan unbuttoned his white shirt sleeves, rolled them up. He flexed his muscles. Tom and Tony slid off their jackets, tossed them onto a nearby table.

The jig played on. People kept dancing. Smoke hung in the air. The hairs on Jonathan's arms caught the light from the spinning, overhead ball.

I tried to pass Ted once more. He blocked my way again. People stared. I said, quietly, "Get out of my way, Ted."

"Make me, Jason. Put it right there." He pointed to his jaw.

I pictured, in slow motion, just how it would feel to punch Ted in the jaw, hear it shatter, see blood pour from his nose. I could do it.

Jonathan rubbed his arm, clenched his fists; he was itching for the fight to start. To land a punch or two. I could see he'd picked out the biggest guy for his target. This was my fight, though. He'd respect that. They knew Ted was mine.

The jig was over. The deejay switched to *Don't Take Your Guns to Town, Son.* I remembered Mom's face when she'd picked me up at jail, when she drove me to court. I remembered facing Ginny and Nita's sentencing. I remembered why I was banned from Melissa's life.

And yet, there was Ted, blocking my way. Looking smug. Looking like the perfect target.

Looking smug! Of course.

One punch and I'd land in jail. There'd be no probation

this time for me and my friends. I wouldn't be able to stop them once I'd started. I glanced across the room. Gareen watched me. She'd have to go home alone; she didn't deserve that.

I felt myself grow stronger, stronger. I could really cream him. I knew it.

I kept my hands at my side. It was the hardest thing I'd ever done in my whole life. I hated Ted for making me that mad. For having power over me. I wasn't going to ruin things now.

I wasn't going to let Ted drag me into trouble this time— even if I would look like a fool. There were worse things.

I took a deep breath, forced myself to relax, put my arm around Jonathan's and Tony's shoulders. "Come on, guys. Let's go sit down. There's a bad smell here." They hesitated, but it was my fight. They'd let me handle it in my own way.

We left Ted and his pals standing there, fuming. Vince and Paul joined them. They all stood there together, calling after us, "Yellow bellies. Chickens. Cluck, cluck, cluck."

I held on to Jonathan's arm. If he went after them, I'd have to go, too. I sat next to Gareen. "Hope you're not too thirsty."

She took my hand, held it just hard enough to let me know she cared. "No. Not at all."

"S'pose you think I'm a coward." I looked away from her.

"No. It took guts to walk away. I heard what he did today. Jason, he wants you to break probation. Why do you think he didn't hit first? Then you'd be able to claim self-defence."

I squeezed her hand hard.

"He's leaving." Jonathan watched the door. "I wanted to smash the works of them. Waited for you to make the first move. It was your fight."

Charlotte said, "Gareen's right, Jonathan. That's what he wanted. To see you all in jail. I don't want you back in there."

The cold air curled in around our feet. Old music played and the old people danced all over the place. They had no system. That's not our way.

When a waltz came on, Gareen pulled me up to dance. We nestled into each other, fitting better than ever before. Melissa danced by and I felt Gareen stiffen and pull away. She was tuned in to my moods. Melissa wasn't like that. So why did I want to yank her away from Adam Dunbar?

After that song, I asked Gareen to go outside with me. We put on our coats and went into the chilly night. In the parking lot the cars shone under the lights. They looked like animals settled down for sleep. "Gareen. How do you see me?"

"Hmm. Remember our science project?"

"Mercury."

"Quicksilver. Used to 'win' metals like gold from ore; to make healing ointments. An old, old chemical used by ancients in alchemy." She reached up to rub her fingers over my almost-moustache. I shivered. "Quicksilver. Used to protect against mildew, mold and rot. Used in compounds to detonate high explosives in shells, grenades, torpedoes. It's hard to know which way you'll go, Jason. You'll be very good or very bad."

"We broke a thermometer to see what the quicksilver was like." I put my arm over her shoulders.

"It split into silver, dancing balls. It did the job perfectly while it stayed in the glass channel. On its own, the quicksilver went all over the place." She leaned against me, put her arm around my waist.

"Quicksilver. Potentially dangerous." I didn't want to hurt her. I pulled her closer, felt her hair on my chin.

"Quicksilver. Potentially valuable. I'm betting on the valuable, Jason." She smiled up at me. A warm feeling washed over me. It felt like spring when summer was just about to begin.

I wasn't sure I liked being called quicksilver. But I'd almost ruined everything just a few minutes ago. Ginny had said she believed in me. I was still learning who I was and what I could handle. Maybe Gareen was right.

We went inside. The tape played Bonjovi's *Bed of Roses*. Adam and Melissa were on the floor. Adam was like a programmed robot— made the right moves with the rhythm of a battery-powered toy. Melissa...Melissa moved to the beat like the song was meant for her. Gareen saw me looking.

"Jason, if she came over and asked you to take her home, what would you say?"

I wanted to say, "I'd tell her to get lost." The words stuck. I never answered.

"You came pretty close to wiping the floor up with Ted, didn't you?"

I wanted to say. "Not really. I've got more sense than that." I couldn't. Not yet. I took Gareen's warm, strong hand.

She nodded like she understood. "Quicksilver." She smiled at me. "Ah, sometimes this old tree feels like crashing down on the two of you. I can't pretend to be friends with Melissa any more. I sometimes think you're not worth having around."

"You promised," I said.

"I know. I promised. And a preacher's daughter keeps her promises. No matter what, we'll be friends."

The music kept on playing. I pointed to the dance floor. We walked hand in hand to hold each other under the spinning ball. Coloured pieces of light showered us. Music poured through me.

I didn't know what would happen next week, next month, tomorrow. For now I was where I wanted to be—even if it hurt a little to see Melissa dance past, in Adam Dunbar's arms. Maybe if I hadn't been easy-led last July...maybe if I kept my nose clean from here on out, Melissa's parents would ease off. I shouldn't think like that, not while I held another girl. A better girl than Melissa. Quicksilver...maybe I'd find my channel...maybe I'd make my channel...

With my cheek against Gareen's silky hair, with my body close to hers, feeling comfortable, like when you're wearing your favorite old sneakers or shoes, I looked around the dance floor. We turned in slow circles.

Joey was there; he held Doreen close enough but not too tight. They looked right together. His eyes shut as they danced together. He was lost in the feel of it all. Like always.

Mike stood at the bar, sipping Orange Crush. He was all alone and watching. Mike looked like his usual worried self.

Tony and Krystal, Tom and Karla, they danced together in a set of four. Their circle moved in and out. They looked like a double set of Siamese twins, joined at the shoulders.

Jonathan picked Charlotte up, whirled her around in a move that had nothing to do with the music, everything to do with the way he felt about her. She laughed and kissed him when he set her on her feet.

All around us other couples circled in their own orbits. I knew something about just about everyone on the dance floor. Or thought I did. They thought they knew all about me. That's the way of small towns. That's funny. Probably no one really knew the truth about anyone else.

Tom let Krystal go, formed a line. He picked up Joey and Doreen, Jonathan and Charlotte. Jonathan led us up to the bar to get Mike. Jonathan took Mike's glass of Orange Crush, put it on the counter, dragged him with us out to the dance floor. Tony put his arms around Mike's shoulders.

We all formed a circle. We danced to Ace of Base's *I Saw the Sign* nice and fast, kicked up our heels, let our energy explode. We kept the circle going for another three dances.

Melissa and Adam danced near us. For a minute I thought they might join us. I might get to put my arm around her shoulders or her waist. She glanced across the room. From a corner, her mother glared at her. Melissa frowned and stayed dancing with Adam the Robot. They stayed apart from our gang.

Charlotte checked her watch. "Twelve o'clock. Almost curfew time." We stayed together in our circle for one more dance. We split for a final waltz. Jonathan and Charlotte kept Mike with them.

I called three taxis from the bar. The music played on, but for our gang it was closing time.

Acknowledgements

Thank you to Shana Cooper who made me write this book by asking each day for the next chapter.

Martin Ware, Anne Murray and her young writers, Jean Gosse, Gerri King, Sara Young, members of the Page One writers group and WANL, Jane Frydenlund, and other writers and listeners who made comments and suggestions to help the story ring true.

Victoria Young for my photo and instructions to tell the story like a young person.

ABOUT THE AUTHOR

D. Jean Young lives and works in Deer Lake, Newfoundland. Writing has been a part of her life for many years and she has had short stories and articles published in magazines. At work, Jean helps people make financial planning decisions, and, at home, she lives with and learns from her husband, three children, and two cats and a dog. *Quicksilver Summer* is her first novel.

010601- DBCN - BAO-3837